SYN

MALCOLM HOLLINGDRAKE

To Steve

Best wishes.

Malcolm

This edition produced in Great Britain in 2021

by Hobeck Books Limited, Unit 14, Sugnall Business Centre, Sugnall, Stafford, Staffordshire, ST21 6NF

www.hobeck.net

A CIP catalogue for this book is available from the British Library.

ISBN 978-1-913-793-29-6 (pbk)

ISBN 978-1-913-793-28-9 (ebook)

Cover design by Jem Butcher

www.jembutcherdesign.co.uk

Printed and bound in Great Britain

❀ Created with Vellum

ARE YOU A THRILLER SEEKER?

Hobeck Books is an independent publisher of crime, thrillers and suspense fiction and we have one aim – to bring you the books you want to read.

For more details about our books, our authors and our plans, plus the chance to download free novellas, sign up for our newsletter at **www.hobeck.net**.

You can also find us on Twitter **@hobeckbooks** or on Facebook **www.facebook.com/hobeckbooks10**.

Dedicated to
Barbara and Don Hackworth and family

Remember you chose to seek out a different place.

The Wizard of Oz

PROLOGUE

Yet again sleep is a ghost as the thoughts of a previous late evening refuse to leave my mind; they replayed like a short horror film and I felt the same flutter of fear at each rerun. The memories tumble like angry surf on a shingle shore, disturbing any chance of relaxation or sleep. It was as if all else had rolled away, like those moving pebbles that seemed to create a cacophony.

The more these thoughts prevail, the more the anger and a deep, deep, resentment are stirred. There had been no need for the rudeness and certainly not the aggression. I had not been eager to get into the bar, nor was I aware of the people to my right who had congregated to the far side of the pavement. The group was loud but the noise seemed to demonstrate their seemingly drunken good spirits. An obvious joke was followed by immediate and intense laughter. One particular female's laugh broke above the rest, high-pitched and scream-like. As she stepped backwards, she collided before finally stepping on my foot. I can still feel the pain the sharp heel inflicted. When I looked at my shoe there seemed to be no obvious harm done, apart from the deep scuff on the brogue's leather. The accidental contact brought an instant turn of her head and her laughter quelled immediately, her hand moving to her mouth in surprise and apology.

'Sorry,' she giggled before stepping and swaying drunkenly back towards the group. A helping hand reached out drawing her within the fold.

I remember her words perfectly. In the next frame of the memory things seemed to slow down, like the images in an old stuttering movie. Each face became crystal clear, each word carved into stone, accompanied by the sound of a fairground organ. Its haunting tones had been barely audible. Then I had felt the firm hand against my shoulder and the strength of the grip that seemed to pull me off balance.

'Fucking hell. Watch where you're bloody going, you clumsy sod! Are you all right love?'

The large, intimidating young man glared at me as he collected the woman and pulled her to one side. His words slurred, and were filled with aggression. Flecks of saliva raced from his lips with every expletive.

She spoke immediately, a referee of sorts. 'It was my fault, Bill. Leave it.' Her voice was commanding, sharp and direct.

The group had gone quiet and the atmosphere became immediately charged by the man's vicious actions and tone. It was as if it were a signal to draw all of the group's attention onto the one man, the stranger, the new victim – me. I know my face showed my anxiety, fear and confusion. But what was on my face was the tip of the anguish that went much deeper within me. My situation was suddenly exacerbated as I saw elbows nudge others. Those within the group seemed to know the script by heart, knew just what was coming next, as if it had happened before, and frequently. Each was preparing for the coming storm.

'Oh *fuck!* Here we go again. Hold tight!' someone chuckled before giving the man called Bill more room.

Bill pushed forward towards me but the woman's hand moved equally as quickly. 'Leave it! It was my fault and you lot, keep it shut!'

In this dream I am now hovering and looking down on the same scene. I remember clearly that at this point a sudden fear flushed through my stomach, bilious and muscle-numbing bringing a burning, tingling sensation to my neck. I am not a fighting man and at that key moment the woman turned and smiled at me. Her expression was not the sarcastic, demeaning grin of the other woman in the group who raised her little finger and waggled it tauntingly. There was concern and kindness within that smile; a tenderness and an apology.

'Sorry. Please go. He'll not touch you.'

She moved her body between us, forcing away his arm and the threatening link that bound us. I remember the sudden silence that hung like a foul stench, and then out of the blue someone repeated the joke's punchline that had started the altercation. Laughter broke out again immediately ridding the atmosphere of tension and anger as if he had come full circle. The woman, one hand on Bill's chest, laughed but not with the same intensity as before. She swiftly raised herself on tiptoe and pushed her face into his before planting a kiss on his lips. It was as if she were sucking the anger from his extended chest and his posture and bravado were immediately deflated. I remember the laughter increasing, and all eyes suddenly moved away. I was no longer the centre of their unwanted attention. The memory went back to real time along with the decreasing nervousness within my stomach as the music faded to a whisper and then was gone. Yet the dream continued. I knew it by heart. Just a different location.

3

Inside the bar it was busy but I remember finding the only quiet corner. I took my drink and sat. My nerves were still unsettled.

I had never been one for confrontation. I could never fight, never wanted to, never saw the point. I would flee rather than fight. I had always been like that – cowardly, some might say.

I can remember the cold bitter taste of my beer, which was not one of my favourites. The noise around me was a cocktail of music and human conversation which grew more inaudible as I sat with my own thoughts for company.

I remember throughout my school life I would seek out the meek and the quiet, often finding friendship more acceptable with the girls than the boys within the classes. The move from primary to secondary school, I recall, had been particularly traumatic. It had brought with it sleep deprivation and severe anxiety. The stories I had heard seemed so real. 'Initiation' was a word I was unfamiliar with one day, but it filled my imagination the next and tormented me throughout the summer holidays before secondary school began. 'They' will put your head down a used toilet before flushing it, I was told. 'They' will get you in a quiet corner, remove your trousers and paint your dick green before putting your clothes in another area of the school.

Who were these people? Who were those known as 'They', the aggressors, the faceless and yet soon to be the familiar. After all, they would be dressed the same as me: same trousers, same blazer, same tie – just bigger, stronger and more cruel. I had heard that it was nothing to do with who you were but purely because you were new. It was nothing personal and when it happened the crowd yelled, 'Just do it, go on, do it!' It was not a judgement, purely a rite of passage.

That summer the words, 'nothing personal', were written large on a piece of red card and added to my bedroom wall beneath my poster of Jean-Claude Van Damme. As I stared into the eyes of the man in the poster, I was determined to fight back. If they were to hurt me, then I would hurt them. If they embarrassed me, I would do the same to them. I, however, would do it in a more subtle way, using not brawn but brains. I recalled the exact moment when I realised that I knew I would always be intimidated and frightened by such people. It was also the time I vowed I would chase them down, flush them out from whichever class, group or gang to which they belonged. Being different, I was aware that I would always be the mouse to their cat but I would, in time, also be the phoenix and rise up for revenge. The mouse would turn and it would roar ... quietly! When I sought revenge, I would add the name to the wall and follow it with a tick.

On that night, in the pub a female's laughter had broken my reminiscing. It was familiar. I looked across the bar, my face flushed and my heart rate increased as the group I had encountered outside moved en masse towards the bar. Lifting my mobile phone from the table I set it on video before lowering my face. A few moments, that is all I would need until all of the faces were captured.

The images in my mind began to fade before turning to black. The whole memory went back to the start only to begin again. I awoke with a start. Sweat bathed my body. The light of the early morning barely penetrated the blinds and I knew for certain that sleep would now be impossible. Climbing out of bed I went to the kitchen. I needed tea.

CHAPTER 1

The high-pitched wail seemed almost smothered, trapped like her arms as the noise grew in volume and intensity. In that moment she had lost all sense of time and place. It was real and confusing and she continued to struggle before realising the truth.

In all humans, the critical moments between sleep and consciousness vary, those precious seconds affect us each in different ways as a dream or nightmare is interrupted by the screaming alarm. Skeeter was no different. Often, these moments are a juxtaposition of dark and light, catalepsy, and a sudden, physical movement of extending an arm from under cover to grope, locate and kill the intrusive noise. That very moment when fingers search and the offending article is found, questions are asked, nay demanded … Why now? Why me?

It was at this precise moment that Skeeter Warlock brought memory and experience into focus to overcome the serious desire to close her eyes, if only for another second. She knew the end result of that. It was sheer willpower that forced her to drag her reluctant frame from the warm sanctuary of her bed.

She believed that five in the morning in May had some benefits. It was light at least, and there was only a slight chill in the air. Possibly a light frost would coat grassy areas in hidden hollows, but in general, the hour was acceptable. However, the warmth of, and the inviting smell from the bedsheets, that recent nest of security, still seemed the better option.

Shift your body, Wicca, you lazy arsed good-for-nothing, and get into your running gear ... now! The instruction, inaudible to the real world, was as clear as the alarm call that had shocked her into consciousness but a few moments before. She was ready to accept the start of her day.

It had been said by many that she was a bit of a machine when it came to the art of physical exercise. Her body was fine toned, sinewy like a bowstring pulled taut. There was no fat on her, only muscle. Her movements exhibited a general aura of health, as seen in her face and eyes. The fact they were so visibly different distracted the onlooker from staring for too long. One was almost black, the other was the most vivid of blue, like that of a robin's egg. This made for a disconcerting contrast.

To place a finger on her wrist and read her resting heart rate would verify the fact that here was a woman in peak physical condition. She strapped on the heart monitor just below her sports bra and checked it against her watch. Moving to the kitchen, she drank a small amount of water. She knew the route she would take. They were planned by the days of the week. The diary chart showed her run the previous Tuesday, along with the weather and her time.

There was often an expletive-filled note at the end of every entry: *Bugger the wind! Poxy rain!*

Running down Bank Brow was particularly slow as her cold muscles made a brief but angry protest. Once into her stride and on the level, she began to find her pace.

* * *

The western sky was still deep navy, smudging and blending invisibly with the horizon, beyond his ability to comprehend it as a visual reference. The sky, to the east, by contrast, high above the flat, sandy sea grass broke into ultramarine and orange; the occasional cut, sliced blood red. The breeze was a whisper. Mist hung in the dip to the side of the road, a grey, cottony veil stretching towards Southport's Pier in one direction and the man-made mounds in the other. The vapour seemed languorous and settled, wanting to remain and defend those artificial barricades. That would be false hope. The advent of the sun would bring warmth, to rip and slough the grey mist's skin from hollows, cracks and crevices. Only night's calling card of heavy dew on a salt-laden land would be left. This daily act of natural destruction – nature's creative hand – would go largely unnoticed.

The sea at Southport was some distance from the coastal road, leaving acres of flat, grey-green sand patched with a camouflage of coastal flora and fauna. It was a bird watcher's paradise and for the next hour it was Trevor's – alone and unseen.

Unzipping the box, Trevor removed the drone, unfolded the legs methodically as he always did before checking each rotor was free. There were eight blades in all, two to each leg. To him, it always looked like a crouching dog. After slotting in the battery, he pressed the button on the belly of the craft – once, twice before the five LED lights flashed in turn. The machine twitched, energised and resurrected. The control pad was connected to a small iPad and with the starting of the app, it synchronised the two. This part of the process he liked. It was clean and ordered. There was no rushing or fuss. It was clinical and effortless; in some ways professional.

At this stage, the drone was learning where it was on the earth, calibrating its compass and preparing for flight. When it was ready it would announce the fact to Trevor that 'the home point had been updated' clearly and precisely. The drone was now ready. Checking a full 360 degrees he ensured the area was safe to fly and that he was alone amidst a huge expanse of flat nothingness. He was ready for the drone to take to the air for the first time that morning. As it lifted, the whine of the rotors chopped the cool air, the new noise flushing a flock of gulls from an area closer to the distant water, to take flight as if in competition.

The small white box printed with a coronet sat on the table, the lid open revealing the contents. The blades, individually wrapped in transparent bags, held a dull sheen but an extremely sharp edge. I carefully brought one out and held it up to catch the light, the curved edge facing uppermost. Sliding it from the packet I inserted the blade into the craft knife handle. I held the old car mat and lowered the blade to meet the edge. One slow pull down saw the carpet begin to separate. I sliced each tough strand, the warp and

the weft surrendering to my touch, separating in one clean, slicing motion. The carpet fell in two pieces to the floor and I quickly changed the blade.

I had stuck the large watermelon onto the section of broom handle which I then trapped in the vice. It looked like a head on a pole – I had given it eyes, ears and a mouth using black felt pen. Holding the new blade inches away from the right ear, I plunged it in as deep as possible before dragging it forward, slicing a clean gash in the fruit's flesh. Juice dribbled from the cut. In the satisfaction of the moment, I lowered my head and ran my tongue along the oozing gash.

CHAPTER 2

The trek along the canal from Appley Bridge to Parbold was one of Skeeter's favourite runs. The River Douglas meandered lazily to the left, often appearing before turning to hide within trees and steep banks. Apart from the song of the early birds the quiet countryside was idyllic. Turning her wrist, she checked her heart rate monitor before moving off the towpath and heading along the farm track. Within fifteen minutes she would be pounding along Lees Lane before facing the gruelling Bank Brow to finish. It was an ascent that seemed to drain every ounce of her determination but filled her with a superior sense of satisfaction on reaching the summit. Leaning on the gate to her cottage she breathed deeply.

'You'll kill your bloody self one of these days, lass. Running's for the guilty and the stupid and you don't look like either to me.' The voice erupted from the far side of the dividing hedge.

It was usually the same words, if he happened to be out early, and she chuckled. 'So you keep advising.'

A plume of grey cigarette smoke escaped from his nostrils and drifted into the air. It appeared like a small, fast disappearing ghost rising mysteriously over the hedge as if signalling a new pope had been selected.

'Taking the air, Tom?'

He chuckled; her sarcasm was not lost. 'Kind of. Wife doesn't allow it inside now the decorators have been.' He moved to where there was a gap in the foliage and winked at Skeeter before inhaling again.

'We'll have to stop meeting like this, Tom.'

'Early morning liaisons. That's a wicked thought to an old fella,' he chuckled to himself. 'I used to run a bit in my time. Not like you. Track stuff. Wigan Harriers when there was a stadium on Woodhouse Lane. All houses now, and before you were born. Happy days. Used to smoke then too, it seemed everyone did. Advertised them on the telly as being cool as mountain streams or made out you'd turn into a cowboy if you smoked enough of a certain brand.'

More smoke filtered across the divide and Skeeter raised her nose allowing it to linger near her nostrils. The aroma was neither strong nor unpleasant. It soon vanished. Even so, she could never understand why people smoked, not now when one considered the financial cost.

'Are you in work today, Skeeter?' He stood and flicked the cigarette butt onto the road.

'For my sins, Tom, for my sins.' She smiled and raised a hand before walking down the path to the cottage door.

* * *

Skeeter glanced right as she turned down Copy Lane. The Victorian style blue police lamp mounted by the door was clearly an anomaly, an anachronism set against the façade of the sixties' architectural brashness. Within minutes, she entered the carpark to the rear. Grabbing her belongings, she made her way in. The welcome was warm and cheery. She was aware that on completion of the new station constructed on the old airport site at Speke, they might not be at the present site for much longer.

'A good early morning, DS Warlock.' The officer behind the desk smiled as he moved away returning with a lanyard and key pass. Checking the photograph on the swinging card he looked up. 'You're getting younger by the day, ma'am. Must be working here that does it!' He grinned as he scanned the code into the system.

Skeeter leaned over and grabbed it. 'Witches never age. They do, however, have the power to lift the spirits of anyone they meet. Seeing you're usually a grumpy sod when on this shift, the magic must be having the desired effect.' Slipping the lanyard over her head, she returned the grin and moved towards the door.

A reorganisation of the open-plan workspace had taken place over the last month and she and her desk had been promoted next to the window. Just above was a written sign: 'Sod all view'. It had been there as long as she could remember and it was true. To compensate she had suspended a small stained-glass window, made by her boss as a thank-you gift after successfully solving a case. The hues, when the sunlight caught it, spread across her desk offering a magical splash of colourful drama.

Within seconds of her sitting down, a paper dart floated into her peripheral vision and landed to the left of her desk.

'You're improving, Tony. More Bleriot than Bader, I think.' She stood but could not see him.

Popping his head round one of the new blue dividing panels he grinned. 'Who the bloody hell are they when they're at home?'

Skeeter shook her head. 'Pilots, Tony. What do you want?'

'Just a morning greeting. Being friendly, like. Tear anyone to pieces at that wrestling club of yours last night?'

Skeeter had been a member of a Wigan wrestling club since she was a child. It enthralled her. She loved the discipline, the technical aspects and the sheer hard work, attributes that had drawn her to becoming a copper. Her father and grandfather had been members of the wrestling club too, one going back to Riley's time. During this period no women were allowed and even the thought of the fairer sex within the club would have brought revolt. Its reputation had grown as more and more wrestlers became world famous. Times had changed and the women now played a key role. Skeeter had the heart of a lion and she sported a number of scars to prove it. The cauliflower ear gave her appearance a certain gravitas – she looked, as they say in the north, hard, dead hard. Certainly, what you saw was what you got. She was also tattooed with her favourite motto, a code she lived and worked by: *By any available means or method.* The words were written in Latin, hidden but always present.

She laughed. 'Training night with the *Tumble Tots*, the kids. Great fun and it takes me back to my first days at the club. I was just going to sort out the paperwork for the wagon theft from Brintonwood Trading Estate until your attempt at making and flying Concorde crashed at my feet.' She chuckled. 'Trailer found empty and should've been full of white goods. The cab? My experience tells me it'll be on its way through Europe by now. Then we've a missing person, young woman, if twenty-eight is still considered young. Seeing the boss in ten.'

Detective Inspector April Decent read through the files for the fourth time. She added the name Carla Sharpe to a white board positioned on the wall to her right before tagging in the date and the time she was last seen. She glanced at the clock on the far wall. April had been with the Merseyside Force for just short of five months. Although there was an initial fear and concern that she had made the wrong career choice, she soon discovered her team was equally as efficient as the one she had been part of in Yorkshire. She had formed a particularly strong bond with Skeeter, her sergeant in Serious Crime. Here was a colleague she could rely on and the more she discovered about her, both professionally and personally, the more impressed she was. At that moment she heard the tap on her door.

'Come in.'

Skeeter popped her head round the door and pushed it open before bending to collect the second mug of coffee from the floor.

'Brought coffee.' She raised her eyebrows.

April pointed to the chair. 'Spitting feathers and ready for one. Thanks. I believe we've traced the stolen goods from the trading estate?'

'Routine stop on the M6 south. Two vans. However, the trailer's long gone. Passed the details to Tony who tells me

Michael will chase up the loose ends when he's in later. He'll do all the boring bits, the links with the continent and the border force.'

DC Michael Peet always worked the late shift. It had become a habit that he relished. The station was quiet then and there was more quality time to put the cases into perspective. He could think, apply logic. If it were a puzzle, a conundrum, then he was the man with whom to leave it. His ambition had always been to enter law. He had the academic and mental agility to be a barrister but his partner, falling pregnant in their second year at university, put a stop to that. Originally, it was to be a temporary suspension of ambition but Murphy's Law was swiftly applied and he found himself with a second and then a third child. As luck would have it, he was now more content than at any previous time in his career. His entry to the force had been to him a retrograde step but those above him in the force had swiftly seen his true potential. He had a clear and full understanding of the law; he was unpretentious and wrestled challenges with determination. Importantly, he was not one to concede. His love for the job was evident.

CHAPTER 3

His hand worked quickly, scribbling the details of the items of clothing into the note pad, paying particular attention to the colours. To be successful, he had to be precise in all respects to give the overall impression that nothing had changed. The fluorescent coat was easy and even the goggles he could find at any DIY store. They could be re-used should the need arise. Blue trousers and wellington boots, it seemed too easy. The clothing should not be new and if it were, it would be purchased outside the area. He would buy at different times at different shops. He took four more photographs using the zoom to highlight the details. He had no need to leave the car and certainly it would be careless to walk too near. The measurement of height and general size was less important. They were what they were, and he could not change that. Last on the list were three CDs – he would find these at a charity shop. Choosing their titles would make for an interesting game.

A tractor droned some distance away as he looked out across the newly planted field to spot the offending article.

There was something relaxing about agricultural toil, something honest. The birds, white against the grey sky, seemed to dance behind the piper. The smell of newly ploughed soil permeated the car and he took a moment to savour the peace before turning to concentrate on the booklet he had retrieved from the glovebox. His fingers flicked over the pages one at a time. Each held a photograph. There were five. The candid images were slightly blurred, screen captures from the video he had taken, but they were clear enough. They had, after all, returned repeatedly night after night in his dream. They were as familiar as family. He remembered each with a certain clarity. Three were male, two were female. What tied each to the next? Each one had been captured staring at the camera but it was clear from their expression that they were unaware that they had been snapped. This was all part of the game.

The dashboard clock showed 6.56am. It was time to leave. He had work to do.

* * *

Tracking the man had been easy. Watching the group's familiarity with one of the bar staff had been convincing enough and once they had left; he had managed a quiet word. Pretending he knew their faces yet being unable to recall their names had brought the answers he needed: Cameron Jennings and Bill Rodgers. He could visualise both but Bill's features filled his mind. He was the one of the pair who would wait. It was Cameron, the person on the outside of the group, the shorter of the two, he wanted to focus on for now. Facebook was the next call and sure enough with that one search he had the group. They were all friends. Finding the place of work for one came as an additional bonus; he had not expected to be so lucky. A female too, Carla Sharpe, was the perfect way to begin.

He could not remember seeing fear like it. The tears, the dribbling snot that ran over the roughly tied material that brought a rictus type grin to what was a pretty face. It exposed her teeth and gums spreading her mouth wide. Mascara had run in two rivulets down either cheek before ending at the mouth. He had taped both arms to those of the director's chair. Her feet locked round either leg before tape secured them in place. It had been an astute thought in the planning to bracket the chair's legs to the garage's concrete floor. He really did not want his guests to leave or move without his consent. Milky grey light spread throughout the room; it was only an adequate illumination but it sufficed. The dirt covered window, opaque and wired was more to keep people out than allow the day to enter.

Strangely, there was no recognition initially, not a glimmer but as soon as she heard him say the words, *Leave him Bill, it was my fault,* there was a moment of understanding. As to the specific occasion she was clearly uncertain. It seemed that this experience with the group that night, with Bill turning aggressive, was such a common occurrence that one would easily blend with another.

'Is Bill always like that, Carla?'

Her eyes opened wider on hearing her name and she snorted, the porcine utterance deep and filled with fear.

'It wasn't my fault but you knew that. You laughed. I know you did. I was there, the innocent stranger. You hoped Bill would perform his party trick and you laughed at my fear, my anguish. What normally happened, Carla? Let me guess. Bill's a bit of a bully. Handy with his fists. Drinks a lot and then can't control his inner demons and he strikes out at whoever upsets him or insults one of the group. Maybe he defends you, Carla. You and the others think it's fun to watch. You had no compassion that night, you demonstrated no human kindness. You did nothing. I've always been bullied. There is one thing that I am though. Unlike Bill, I'm patient. It took a while to find you. Time to plan when I could take you without being seen. You made it easy. Headphones on and running alone on the same route. It was perfect – you actually believed me when I stopped you. I have that kind of face, my mother always said so.' He turned briefly to see himself in the mirror hanging on the wall. 'Sorry, Carla. Now, to what were you listening?'

Without removing the gag, she could not answer. He lifted her mobile, took her finger and activated it. 'Let's just have a look before we change your print entry to a password. Now look at that. How apposite. You were listening to something called 'Dark Lane Demo Tapes' by Drake whoever he or she is.' He listened to one of the tracks holding her headphones to his ear before moving it to hers. 'A male voice I think.'

'Was it this you were listening to?'

She nodded feverishly.

'You'd nod at the moon if I asked right now, girl. If I were in your shoes then so too would I.' He leaned over and his hand patted hers. 'In a minute I want you to do as I say. Nod if you understand.'

Carla's frightened eyes looked towards his as tears rolled down the dark mascara avenues.

* * *

Skeeter drained the final dregs of coffee from her mug allowing it then to swing on her finger whilst she looked at the file notes. 'I see she has a record. Not exactly the world's worst criminal though.' She slipped the mug onto the desk. 'Drunk and disorderly at Aintree Ladies' Day weekend last year. How many have been guilty of that little faux pas? And reported by a witness as having been involved in an altercation on a Saturday night outside the *Blue Boar* on Lord Street, Southport, six months ago.' She flicked over the page. 'A beauty therapist, whatever that means, and she's single. Twenty-eight and single?'

April just watched Skeeter whilst using her two fingers as drum sticks to tap out a muted rhythm on the edge of the desk. Skeeter turned. 'Once worked with a bloke who used to play a desk. He'd put on some piano music, walk up to his desk as if he were approaching a grand piano and pretend to flick the tails on his coat. He'd do all the stretching exercises with his fingers and then mime away, all the finger and hand flicking, but what used to crack me up was his facial expression. Each note produced a different face. He was great fun. Good copper too. Was killed trying to stop a stolen car.'

April stopped playing. 'I was enjoying your story until the last sentence. Finger tapping? A habit that seems to help me think.' She looked at her hands.

'Getting run down? All part of the job on the thin blue line. I see we have an address. Was anything found there?'

'Apparently she came out of a long-term relationship about nine months ago. Moved to her present address. Trying to get access from the landlord. We've contacted the ex-partner, Callum Smith. He'd heard she'd gone missing from Carla's friend, Debbie Sutch, the person who called us. She'd been ringing round and believed she might have gone back to him. Apparently, she missed a lunch appointment with her. This friend, had called at her flat when she failed to turn up and she couldn't contact her by phone. Smith was interviewed but he hadn't seen her for a month or so. He lives in Upton on the Wirral. Works as a yoga teacher and personal trainer. No previous record with the police.'

'Is there a number for him?' Skeeter turned, grinned and winked. 'Just asking for a friend like.'

They both giggled.

'According to Sutch, Carla was well in herself. Enjoyed her work and socialising. Apparently, she'd given up men apart from, and I quote: "the occasional quick shag".'

Skeeter immediately turned to look at April. 'That can be a dangerous game, especially if she changes her mind at the last minute. Do we have any names?'

April shook her head.

'And the last …' Skeeter didn't finish.

'According to Debbie they were together the evening before, drink and an Italian meal.' April checked the file. '*Presso* on Lord Street by the Cenotaph. She even dropped her at her flat. Carla had been working late. They met at eight. They were meant to be lunching the following day so unless she went out afterwards … Sutch was the last person to see her. We have an officer checking with the neighbours now.'

'Did Carla have any set routines?' Skeeter enquired flicking deeper into the file.

'Like you, she ran. According to Debbie Sutch she jogged

most mornings before work. Obsessed with the fear of losing her figure as she got older, allegedly. Work was normally a 10am start but she wasn't working the day they were meeting for lunch. She was unsure as to whether she exercised on her day off.'

'Nothing else? Gym, coffee shop?'

April shook her head. 'Not that we know.'

'List of other acquaintances? Friends, work colleagues?'

April slid a sheet of paper over the desk. 'Both. I want you and Tony to call at *Nic's Nails and Beauty*, and I've sent Lucy Teraoka and Fred Quinn to interview her friends. There's one in particular I'm very interested in.' She collected a drumstick from the in tray, leaned over and let the tip fall on one name. 'William Rodgers. Interesting record. In the book for affray five years ago. Criminal offence and served six months. Unusually, and luckily for him, he was tried in the Magistrates' Court. I put the word round and he has a reputation for being a bit of a thug and football hooligan too. Lucy's aware of the need for caution with that one and he's been invited to the station rather than interviewing him at his home. I've planned a briefing for 8am tomorrow to collate what we know. Let's hope Carla's been found before then.'

Skeeter yawned. 'Standard risk in my opinion and not really our bag if I were to be honest, ma'am, but you're the boss. You know she's probably away having it away!' She fluttered her eyes innocently.

'But if she's not. Let's not wing this one. I have a feeling.'

* * *

'Carla, in a moment I want you to stand and I want you to remove your clothes apart from your underwear. You'll remove your upper garments first whilst you remain on the chair. I can assure you that I will turn my back. I am not a sexual predator. I give you my word, so in that sense, you're safe. When that's done I will untape your legs. Then I must trust you.' He paused and stared at her. 'However, if you try to remove the gag I will …' He paused again before moving closer to her face than he had done throughout the kidnap. '… hurt you.'

His face remained expressionless. She felt the warmth of his breath. It was strangely comforting yet at the same time unnerving, making him appear human and real. She watched as he bent and slit the tape holding her arms, noticing the balding ring on the crown of his head.

'You may begin to undress when your circulation returns. I'm sorry for any discomfort.'

Carla hurriedly removed her upper garments and tossed them on the floor next to the chair. He could hear her laboured breathing as only her nostrils could take in the air. The knotted cloth was held tightly in her mouth. It had not moved. She listened when she had done as requested and waited anxiously. She could hear the occasional vehicle some distance away but nothing else.

'Are we done?' Not waiting for an acknowledgement, he turned. 'Good. Now listen to me again. It's critical that you understand and follow my instructions. When you've removed your jeans, you need to put on these clothes and remain standing. Do not move away from the chair.'

Turning, he went to the far side of the room where the diffused light barely filtered before returning with some clothing still in its wrappers. He placed the items before her. 'I want you to put these on. I know they'll be on the large side but that's why we have tape.' He turned away again.

Within minutes she was dressed. 'Don't forget to remain standing.' Turning he looked at Carla. The fluorescent jacket, the peaked baseball cap, the blue trousers and the work gloves were on the large size. He moved forward and lifted the jacket before wrapping tape around her waistband, securing the trousers as tightly as possible. He did the same to her thighs just above her knees as he adjusted the length of the trouser legs. The jacket cuffs he allowed to fall over her hands. The final act was to tighten the cap.

'See, that's better. We still have bits to add but we'll do that later. You look the part I have to admit, Carla.'

Slipping the surgical glove below his wrist, he checked his watch. 'We have time and I think you need a drink. And we need to do something else. We need to ensure that at least one of your friends comes to find you. We have to record a message or two.' He retrieved her phone. 'And to do that, Carla, you must ask some of them to rescue you by recording messages here. Can I trust you just to speak and not shout? We'll soon see.'

He immediately noticed her relax as she sat in the chair before moving her hands hidden within the sleeves of the jacket to her eyes.

'Let's remove that gag for a minute or two and then we can get on.'

CHAPTER 4

Lucy and Fred had managed to contact three of the friends by phone and arranged a time to call. It was important that they meet face to face. It was, as Lucy knew only too well, their responses and facial expressions or the photographs on mobile phones that could hold vital clues, help differentiate between truth and lies. These nuances could easily be missed during a phone interview. Meeting face to face was heavy on resources but invaluable.

Their first meeting with Cameron Jennings went as planned. The reports confirmed what they already knew about Carla. Lucy jotted down as part of his statement something that seemed a little bizarre. It was one of Carla's favourite sayings, 'Life is for living – just live it!' It seemed to be an irony. According to Cameron, it was written on one of the walls of her flat, and she wondered why he had drawn her attention to that. He also informed them that she had gone missing once before – two days in the Lake District. It was to help her overcome an upset. What that upset was he was unsure.

* * *

Tony entered *Nic's Nails and Beauty* first and the woman behind the work station peered at them over her glasses, the white protective face mask covering her mouth and nose. She called out for assistance. A man in his early twenties came out from behind a beaded curtain. He walked, toes in, taking small but precise steps.

'How may we assist?' His lilting voice was mellow and gentle and seemed to match the pinks and yellow mix of his shirt.

Tony held out his ID. 'That's me, and this is DS Warlock. We'd like to speak with the boss.' Tony's voice seemed to have dropped an octave as if in contrast to that of the assistant. Skeeter chuckled internally understanding his psychology.

'Please,' Skeeter added and then smiled.

'I'll be at least fifteen minutes,' the person working on the nails called. 'If you're happy to wait. This is my last client today. Carlos, offer our guests a drink.'

Both refused. As Carlos left, Tony turned to Skeeter, pulled a face and mouthed 'Carlos?'

It was twenty-five minutes before Nicola slipped the mask from her face and dropped it in the bin. Skeeter watched her stretch and then rub the small of her back before moving across to the waiting area.

'Sorry, took longer than I thought. How can we help? Any news of her? It's not like her this is it Carlos?'

A distant voice called back like an answering echo. 'Not at all. Regular as the Atkinson Gallery clock is our Carla.'

'May I have your full names, please?' Skeeter asked whilst

opening her notepad.

There was a pause as if she was not expecting the question. 'Yes, sorry. I'm Nicola Turner and that's Brian Briggs. We call him Carlos as he always copied the way Carla worked when he first started with us.'

Carlos popped his face through the beads. He blushed.

'Can you tell us how Carla was on the day she worked late, the day before she went missing, a Wednesday? Her physical and mental state? That was the last time you saw her, yes?'

'Yes. It was a normal day, busy, but then midweek we can be. She chatted about meeting Debbie. We know Debs don't we, Carlos? She seemed her usual carefree self.'

Carlos parted the beads again. 'Lovely lady is Debs. Great fun, as is our Carla.'

'So, the last time you saw her was when she stepped out of that door to go home?' Tony asked whilst pointing.

Carlos slipped back behind the screen as if he did not want to answer.

'Yes. Thursday's always her off day. If we're busy she'll usually help out and work. She's been with me for a few years now. Reliable, professional and you could say, a friend.'

'We know about a failed long-term relationship. Did that cause any issues as far as work was concerned? We know she moved house too. Did she need time off?'

'He was a bit of a dick to be honest. Treated her like a rubbing rag. Handsome bugger though. He was playing away a lot, his clients she told us. I knew it to be a fact. One was another of my friends. Carla had given him a number of chances. He'd send flowers when he was guilty and she'd soon turn and run back to him.'

'Do you know if there was any violence?'

'No, she'd have said. She was more likely to give him a thick ear ...' She stopped as she glanced at Skeeter's cauliflower ear. 'Carla could give as good as she got especially when she'd had a few gins.'

'Life is for living – just live it!' The raised voice from the back called swiftly followed by Carlos's face. 'Her motto, her mantra for a happy life.'

'Neither of you have heard from her nor seen her since the evening she left here?'

Skeeter repeated Tony's question but this time concentrated on Carlos's expression.

He shook his head.

Nicola immediately chipped in. 'As I said to you earlier. No.'

The interview was quickly wound up and Tony requested Carla's client list for the last twelve months to be mailed through to the station. He handed her a card containing his contact details.

'I'd like to photograph your appointment diary for this month so we can start to check against your CCTV.' He removed a memory stick and placed it on the table between them. 'I need you to copy all recordings made the week prior to Carla's last day and disappearance. We need you to keep anything else you have until notified. Is that clearly understood?'

Nicola was taken aback but agreed. She went to the desk returning with the diary. Tony started to photograph the pages whilst Nicola took the memory stick. On receipt of everything, they left.

The day was clearly retreating as streaks of orange and

yellow blazed the sky. The west coast offered many fiery sunsets at this time of year and tonight's was going to be special.

'Shepherd's delight, Tony. Beautiful colours. Turner would be enthralled.'

Carlos slipped passed them and smiled. 'Hope you find her soon.'

Tony nodded and watched as he turned out of sight before returning his gaze to the sky.

'Right! Shepherds, yes, if you say so. To me it's more like his shirt. That or Hell's mouth! I need a pint.'

'You always do and besides, that was more pink than red. Did you see Carlos's expression when I asked about the last time they'd seen Carla?'

Tony looked at his partner and shook his head, chewing at his thumbnail before spitting the removed section onto the pavement. 'Why?'

'Well, he never actually answered it. He shook his head did our Brian, but he also looked at his boss for guidance.'

'And the point is?'

'A copper's nag, Tony. But what would you know about that? You only care about snagged bloody nails. Filthy ones at that. Don't forget briefing at eight. You can drive me back to the station. I need home, shower and relaxation.'

'I need to give these to Michael. He'll have them processed for the briefing.' Tony held up his phone and the memory stick.

Skeeter smiled inwardly. He might be uncouth but he was very efficient.

CHAPTER 5

He gently removed the drinking straw from the side of Carla's lips. 'It's time, Carla. Did you enjoy the drink?'

Carla nodded. The light entering the room had slowly diminished rendering the far corners dark and invisible. The only bright spot in the room came from an angled torch standing on end some distance in front of the chair. With it came the silhouette and shadows. By her feet was a pair of wellington boots.

'I want you to put these on. They will fit. I'll help if you need me to.' Once on, he taped her arms to the chair again. 'I'll only be a moment.' His words were soft and encouraging. Maybe all this was about to stop. The idea brought a slight flush of excitement to her stomach.

Carla watched as he raised the garage door, the electric motor offering a slight whir. The growing entry allowed the last rays of the day's warm coloured light to slowly creep along the concrete floor into the space. They were welcome. Her captor moved outside ducking below the rising door. It was then that she focused on the car as it reversed into the garage. The smell from the exhaust filled her nostrils. The brightness of the reversing light hurt her eyes as she waited for the brake lights to appear. Only one red light winked on momentarily. Within those few seconds the idea flashed into her mind that this all might be a silly hoax. Were friends playing a joke on her? Would someone suddenly jump out holding a camera and call 'Surprise!'? The thought arrived and disappeared as swiftly as the flash of red light. She watched the driver return. Although she had no idea who this man was, he had, in a strange way, always been considerate and kind. *If this was someone's idea of a bloody joke then they're in for a right bollocking,* she muttered to herself.

The torch light flashed on the blade. Carla watched as it quickly sliced through the tape and she was escorted to the rear passenger seat. He pulled the seat belt over her shoulder before slipping an electrician's tie round her wrist and then through the passenger restraining handle just above the door.

'Comfy? We're going for a ride and then, if you do as you're told I'm going to leave you. Someone will find you because I'll send your friends the message you recorded from your phone. I wonder who'll be the first to come to your rescue? You've been a good girl, Carla. I hope they all come at once.' He smiled and patted her knee again with his gloved hand. 'Retribution you understand. You know the word?'

Carla shook her head.

'I thought not. I know it can seem wrong to seek retribution after the event. I'm sure you're aware that time can heal and it often does, after all, they say it's the universal healer. I'm not so sure. I've thought long and hard about all of this. I want you to know that. Both have a purpose –

retribution and time – both can heal, Carla, but one, I feel, will always leave a scar. Healing and being healed is how we survive as human beings … it's how we move on. You have to destroy to create. You know that saying? Anyway, let's not worry about the rights and wrongs. We've come this far; we should see it through.'

The drive took twenty minutes. The roads grew narrow and twisting and Carla felt the car slow as it pulled to the side of the road and onto a rough track. Beads of sweat had formed beneath the rim of the cap as nausea crept into her stomach owing to the car's motion.

'Do you see him yet, your twin?' The interior was dark but she could sense his excitement.

She watched as his arm pointed to the right side of the car. There appeared to be nothing visible. Allowing her eyes to focus and acclimatise to the dark conditions she could slowly make out a figure towards the centre of the small field. She prayed it would be the person with the camera.

'Do you see him?' He turned and looked at her, an eagerness in his question that was almost childlike. 'No? This will help you. Look now!'

Lifting the small but high-powered torch he shone it through the glass. The focused beam illuminated the object, the figure. At first Carla thought it was a real person, maybe a friend but her optimism soon waned as she realised it was a scarecrow. It was not like you imagine a typical scarecrow to look; as if crucified, arms out, no feet, old clothes blowing in what breeze there was. This was far more sophisticated. It was probably a shop mannequin. The arms were positioned to look as though they were holding a shotgun across the front of their body. The clothes were vivid and bright.

Goggles covered the eyes and a scarf the mouth. The red baseball cap finished the makeover and gave it a human appearance. What really caught her eye was the slowly rotating CDs dangling from the sleeves and waist. The reflective surfaces caught the flashlight beam returning the light as they spun in the breeze.

'This farmer has always fascinated me. He makes and hides the most magnificent scarecrows. Yes, I know you're dressed in exactly the same clothes … as I said, you're twins. Now, Carla, I'm going to ask you to be good just one final time.'

* * *

April Decent had walked Tico, her blue brindle greyhound, along Ainsdale beach. It was a rescue dog, proving to be gentle, loyal and good natured. Initially, he was always on the lead as he was constantly alert. If he saw something in the distance he would be gone. She had been warned that the breed can see things humans cannot and would chase anything moving; even a plastic bag caught by the wind would be fair game. Coming from racing, this new world was very different and he needed time to become accustomed to new experiences and a new way of life. In that respect, he was a bit like her.

Looking at him now, they had both succeeded. Even Sky, the neighbour's Border Collie, had started to accept him. Tico, now curled in front of the wood-burning stove, was the picture of gentleness and peace. His right paw occasionally twitched as if linked to part of his dream. Maybe he was racing again. Who would ever know? April sipped red wine and listened to music. It was a sad song about broken boats by folk duo, The Huers. Their music had been recommended to her. She found it hard to concentrate on it now, and even though the song was beautiful her mind was elsewhere. In all her police career, women going missing without trace always brought to her a strange anxiety. How could someone, unless by their own volition, simply disappear without anyone seeing? In reality it happened frequently, and on many occasions, those missing are never found. They become vapour, ghosts but were more likely modern-day slaves.

She flicked through the notes she had brought home of the missing people logged on the Merseyside website. Age did not seem to play a part, but sex did as there appeared to be more long-term missing females than males. Carla was not the first and neither would she be the last, but she was the first on April's watch. That upset her and made her more determined to find her. Why had this case focused her mind when the assessments had it logged as standard risk? Even Skeeter thought her foolish. She reflected on the word 'standard'. It was a clever way of saying 'low', translated as 'bugger off and stop wasting valuable police time'. Sipping more wine, an advert for condoms came to mind where clever psychology had been utilised within the wording: 'large, medium and trim'. Trim? Nobody would admit to small. She chuckled to herself.

'Where are you Carla Sharpe?' she asked into her glass. 'Where on earth can you be?'

* * *

'In a moment we are going to walk over there. You'll be a good girl and you will take the place of that scarecrow. It's attached to a firm frame, I checked before. Once I leave you, I'll send your photograph and the message to your friends and they can race to find you. They'll check the location I send too.' Shining the torch directly at her he studied her eyes. Everything was written in their green, yet premature rheumy depth. He could see a cocktail of fear and confusion but also a smattering of relief that the ordeal was nearly all over. 'Will Cameron arrive first or will it be Debbie? Maybe it will be Bill? Big, strong Bully Bill.'

Removing the scarecrow from the metal armature he hooked Carla's arms over the horizontal 'T' piece. Producing the Gaffer tape from his pocket, he bound her to it by securing the tape under her armpits. He strapped her to the crosspiece ensuring her body hung like that of the original. Running the tape around her waist he fastened her to the vertical upright. It was clearly a deep-rooted scaffolding pole as it never moved. Suddenly he was hit by a strong and pungent smell that was brought on a gust of wind. It immediately brought death and decay to mind. Shining his torch towards the nearby hedge and allowing the beam to slowly search along its length he saw the cause. The part decaying corpse of a small deer was just visible. Ignoring it he turned back to Carla.

'I told you this farmer made them strong. They're out in all winds and weathers but you, my dear, should be home by morning. That's what friends are for. By the way, sorry for the occasional smell. That's nature for you.'

Removing the goggles from the scarecrow, he slipped them over her cap and then over her eyes. Her world blurred

37

immediately. From his pocket he removed the chosen CDs already prepared and attached to string. They were each placed in the same location as those on the scarecrow. One was affixed to Carla's waist and another to each sleeve. Stepping back, he removed her phone and took two photographs. He checked them. 'That's not too bad, Carla. They'll not drive past. How could they possibly fail to recognise you? You're like the original Dr Syn. You wouldn't know who he was though would you? At my age, neither should I. We are the product of our mother and our father's father if our father is missing from our lives.'

Carla tried to wriggle but the tape proved too secure. The metal pole seemed rigid too. *I'll try harder when he's gone*, she thought. She watched as he carried the scarecrow to the car placing it into the boot before he returned.

'I'm going to leave you in a minute, Carla. You still don't remember seeing me, do you?'

She shook her head.

'You know of our past meeting. I mentioned it when we talked in the garage but let me take you back in time again. Try to remember. You were with your friends. There was Debbie, Bill, Cameron and another. You were standing outside the bar that's in the side road near the Scarisbrick, you know it?'

She nodded frantically, wanting him to just go.

'Good. Someone was telling jokes and an innocent man walked by. Debbie was laughing so much she stepped back and barged into him. Bill decided to become abusive. You thought the fear on the man's face was funny, the others did too. I saw it clearly. Do you remember now?'

After a moment she nodded, this time it was barely visible.

'That stranger, that butt of your laughter, was me. I was that joke of a man. I had done nothing to deserve that. Fortunately, one of your group, Debbie, showed some compassion, some kindness whilst you … that's why you're here and not her. Fear and uncertainty make horrible bedfellows. However, Carla, we met before that. You don't recognise me?' He lifted his hand and extended his little finger. 'You were very drunk. You seemed to know me that night when you laughed again. You did this.' He waggled the digit. 'Remember, your friend saved me. I can see you're confused and frightened, I can tell that. But I didn't recognise you then, it was only later when I saw your face clearly. Now, I see that you're uncertain as to whether I'll do as I've said. What's the saying, Carla? You don't know anyone until you walk in their shoes. You are at this moment metaphorically walking in the shoes I walked in that night, filled with fear and uncertainty of what the next minutes would bring. That's the worst part – the not knowing. Not fun, is it? Those are my wellingtons you wear. Then there was the broken promise and the humiliation – we never like to experience those things, do we?'

She shook her head again and tears began to flow behind the goggles.

'This, Carla, is retribution. You'll remember that word now and you'll remember me.' Leaning closer he whispered in her ear. She twisted her head round to look. He lifted the goggles. 'Yes, it's me.' The smile on his lips was cold but his eyes laughed. Good night, Carla.'

* * *

Copy Lane was busy, even at 7.30am. April moved through to her desk. Four Post-it notes were attached to her computer screen. Each contained a reference search code and each was initialled by Michael. She noticed he had also left a note under the drum sticks.

Went through the requested CCTV last night. I've tagged the customers against the diary for Nic's Nails and Beauty *for the last month. As many numbers and addresses as possible. Any curious links I've highlighted.*

You'll see there are also links to CCTV for the areas between Sharpe's place of work and her apartment and also positioned near Presso. I've linked with the CCTV footage for the day after also – the day she vanished. It's clear she did go for a run. There are three references. The last at 7.45am.

Interestingly, I tracked images of Callum Smith from his social media profile. You might be surprised to see that he called at the salon two days before she went AWOL but there's no reference in the diary so possibly it was a social call?

I checked Carla Sharpe's phone records. They're on file: reference 20/6692/PH. Again, I've highlighted key elements to save you time. The phone's been off since 11am on the day she disappeared. The phone company will notify if it's used.

Sorry I haven't managed more.

When you read this, I'll be dreaming of beautiful things.

Enjoy your day. Good luck.

Michael

PS I've put a request out for dashcam footage for the areas where Carla was last seen running and the predicted route. It's a long shot but at least it's a shot!

The penultimate sentence brought a brief smile, but she swiftly underlined the section noting Callum Smith. It was clear he had lied when questioned. She found the report of the interview. He stated that he had not seen her for a month or so. It was unclear, and now too vague. Picking up the phone, she requested he be brought in for questioning. More murders are committed through estranged relationships, jealousy, vengeance and in some cases, pure anger, than any other motive. April knew she was pushing the limit of her authority as it had been just over forty-eight hours since the missing person report had been logged. She was also aware that this period in a search was critical if Carla had been kidnapped. *People can soon become possible victims,* she thought as her mobile rang. It was DCI Mason, her immediate superior.

'I see we've a briefing at eight regarding a Carla Sharpe? Why, Decent? It's low grade.'

She had only sent him the timetable and the initial reports before leaving the evening before. She neither expected him to be present nor contact her unless, of course, he felt it was inappropriate and a waste of police time and resources at this stage.

'Sir. I'll be co-ordinating the next stage on receipt of the information from interviews done late yesterday afternoon and evening. We'll then be better informed as to the next step. Overnight the CCTV results have been viewed and checked and we have a clearer picture of Carla Sharpe's movements on the day she went missing. We also have an anomaly. A statement given by her last partner doesn't check with CCTV. I've requested he be brought in immediately.'

'Good. I'm presuming from what you say that you've based this on the facts received and not some airy-fairy concern by a member of the public whose friend has failed to meet an appointment? You've done the necessary risk assessments considering the necessary steps and resources management? Or, as I feel from your communication, DI Decent, you feel strongly that she's not just skipped off with some new fella for a few days without telling anyone?' The question was rhetorical; he did not give her time to answer. 'April Decent, just keep me informed and don't embarrass yourself. Do an assessment report with all the new intelligence and get it on my desk as soon as. If you have to up the risk level then go through FIB and do it through the authorising officer. Don't embarrass yourself at this early stage in the bloody game.' The phone went dead.

April felt vindicated and breathed a quiet but shaky sigh.

CHAPTER 6

The sun had broken over the trees at the far side of the field as birds circled before settling on and within the furrows. Two crows chased a lone buzzard, an aerial dogfight set against the misty azure. The smaller adversaries would soon see the buzzard move away, another dawn victory. Wood pigeons busily pecked at the new shoots, oblivious of their guardian standing fewer that ten feet away. The spinning and flashing discs proved to be an ineffective deterrent. The gas driven bird scattering gun set further down the field looked more like a miniature tank than a deterrent. It certainly had the desired effect on the birds but not on the farmer's neighbours who were constantly angered by the early morning blasts. There was a whisper of a breeze and few clouds. In low-lying areas a layer of gossamer-thin frost remained. The dawn chorus had broken early and it would be another hour before those regulars using the lane would pass. It would be unlikely they would note a difference to the regular farm figure. They knew the scarecrow; it had been there a few weeks now and it had brought a smile to those passing. It was one of five dotted around the farm.

The red cap was now tilted to the right. Unless up close it was not easy to see that the exposed right side of the neck gaped cleanly and angrily, almost mouth-like. Below that and over the front of the fluorescent coat ran what appeared to be a deep, red-brown stain. The arms moved in a slight pendular fashion driven only by the slight breeze that was stronger on the exposed field. To the passer-by familiar with the scene, nothing seemed out of the ordinary. It still brought a glance and a smile.

* * *

Cameron Jennings woke with a start as his mobile phone vibrated along the bedside cabinet seconds before the ring tone, the old-fashioned phone bell rang loudly. Lifting his head, he could see the screen had illuminated and cast a hazy green glow in the darkened room. Grasping it, he noticed the call was from Carla's phone. He rubbed his eyes and brought the phone to his ear. He did not give her a chance to speak.

'Bloody hell, Carla, where the fuck are you? We've all been worried sic—'

'I need your help. Now, today. I know it's early. Don't tell the others. Meet me at the start of Ralph's Wife's Lane, the entrance by the footpath. You know the place. Look for a blue car. Now, Cameron, now!'

The voice was unsteady as if she were breathless. He listened and was about to speak when the call ended abruptly.

'Carla! Carla!' he shouted angrily into the void.

With fumbling fingers, he dialled her number but the phone was dead.

Ending the call, Cameron glanced at the time on the phone's screen. Swinging his legs out of bed he went into the bathroom. He tried to put into perspective what he had just heard. What on earth could be the problem, especially considering the time. He laughed, a laugh of realisation when something comes back to haunt, to slap you in the face. He had always believed and preached that true friends never question. Should one of them ring in the middle of the night requesting help you do not ask why. You go. That is what true friends do. *What's round comes around, Cameron,* he said to himself as he splashed water on his face before glancing in the mirror. Bugger the hair, get a cap. He quickly dressed. Unbeknown to himself, he slipped his crew neck jumper on inside out. Grabbing a coat, cap, wallet and keys he prepared to leave. He then remembered his phone. Collecting it, he checked again. There had been nothing since that early call. He knew the spot. He had run the path often. By car it should take him no more than ten minutes. It took eight. Just as she said, a blue car was waiting in the small lay-by.

* * *

Tony and Skeeter were already in the room as Fred and Lucy entered. April would be the last. Tony had placed a fiver on the desk and was already negotiating a bet with anyone who would take it.

'My money's on Carlos Briggs,' he mumbled tapping the note.

Fred looked at Lucy and then at the fiver. He did not get

time to ask. He thought about the evidence – *could she again be in the Lake District and distracted?* He did not commit.

'Morning. First things first. We still have nothing. No sighting nor communication. Nothing from public requests. What we do have is some information from Michael, who's been working overnight on the CCTV and phone records linked with the case. Key to that intelligence is Callum Smith. In his statement he informed us that he hadn't seen Carla for, and I quote, "a month or so". But we have video evidence clearly showing he went to the salon only last week when Carla was present.'

Fred slipped a fiver over Tony's. 'You're on. I'll take Smith.'

April looked up and noticing the money frowned but continued. 'He's due in for further questioning at eleven thirty this morning. Skeeter I want you present. Secondly, we have a list of telephone contacts from those interviewed earlier. Many correspond to the list of friends we already hold. Fred and Lucy interviewed three yesterday and one is due in later today. Fred, you'll be with me for that.'

'Ma'am. Do we have a time?'

'Five.' She pointed to the two fivers on the table. 'Who's gambling on whom?'

'I think Smith and Tony here thinks it's someone called Carlos Briggs.'

'Make that the last time you ever do that in one of my briefings. End of.'

Tony raised his eye brows and looked at Fred before mouthing the word, *Ouch!*

April moved on. 'Carla was last seen on CCTV running along Fairway. She was seen on the camera situated at the

Fairway Park and Ride. There were no other sightings in that area.'

Fred interrupted. 'According to the statements from her neighbours she ran almost daily. Her route was regular. From her flat in Argyle Road she'd run around the perimeter of the golf links and that would include Fairway. Normally about forty-five minutes to an hour. They also said she always ran wearing headphones. Cameron Jennings told me that he occasionally ran with her. According to him, she'd always kept herself fit and did all things right apart from liking a drink or two and sometimes more than a few too many.'

'Noted. Fairway can be a busy area at best.'

Lucy chipped in. 'Along Fleetwood Road close to the links there are some hidden areas of pathway now the trees are in leaf. Have we requested ...'

'Webcam footage has been requested, Lucy. Michael put out the call last night. The likelihood is, if she got into a car, she knew the driver otherwise there would have been a struggle.' April turned back to Fred and Lucy. 'The friends?'

'Everything seemed normal. They tended to socialise regularly. Drinks, meals out. Clubs in Liverpool on occasion. The girls would do more as a collective. However, it would appear she's buggered off before without telling anyone.'

There was an immediate silence. The information came as a body blow to April. Had she responded too quickly in starting the investigation – bolted before the gun? If she had, she would be a laughing stock. Fred turned his attention to the fiver still sitting on the table and mumbled to himself.

'When?' April's voice was shaky and she leaned on the table to regain some equilibrium.

'After one of Smith's affairs. Away for a couple of nights. Contacted no one and they were told when she returned there was no phone signal which I believe. No signal, no communication. According to one friend, I have his name on file, she came home and went straight back to him.'

'Shit!' April's face flushed red for the second time.

'But she's on her own now, ma'am. There's no reason to indicate she'd just go. All the statements I've seen suggest she's more settled and in control than ever.' Lucy's words were judged, professional but more importantly, comforting. 'And this is only my belief – if she's been taken and the perpetrator knew of this previous disappearance it would play into his hands. It would give time.'

April looked around and could see that Lucy's prognosis of the evidence was at best optimistic but probably naïve. Few seemed to give it credence.

'What about this so-called relationship with Callum Smith?'

'On and off for four or so years. They eventually got together. Lived in a flat on Lord Street at that time but when they parted company, she moved into a one bed in Argyle Road. Nice too. According to Debbie Sutch, they were well suited as a couple. Both up for a laugh, neither wanted marriage nor kids, both fitness freaks. Seemed perfect but he liked to stray and she liked the booze. We requested permission to access her phone records and she's been fully co-operative.'

'Lucy, check with the landlord of their old flat. Usual procedure. Damage, nuisance etc. Skeeter, Tony, what about *Nic's Nails and Beauty?*'

Skeeter spoke. 'She was well liked; worked there some

years. Good client list, according to the boss. We've asked for that to be sent through. Her diary for the last month was given to Michael last night, so that's why he's tagged Callum, I guess. As you said, and contrary to his original statement, we now have evidence he was in last week.'

'Before we jump to conclusions.' April glared at Fred and Tony. 'He wasn't in the diary, probably a social call. If they've been an item for years then he could also be a friend of other members of staff. We'll find that out this afternoon. Sorry, you were about to say?'

'There's also another member of staff. Carlos, Carlos Briggs, apparently named after Carla for no other reason than that he learned much from her when he first started. Modelled himself on her ways.'

'Naivety or infatuation?' Lucy asked.

Skeeter just raised her shoulders. 'Something I'm keen to follow up. His real name is Brian Briggs. I ran a check early this morning. No form but I had a nag about him. I think he saw Carla on the day she went missing but that's only my guess.' She explained to the team her rationale.

CHAPTER 7

Lucy parked on Lord Street, Southport. It always amazed her that the gulls' shrill screams seemed to dominate the place but with so many cafés and takeaways the possibility for a free meal was ever present. She had managed to locate and contact the landlord of the property which Carla and Callum had previously rented. The flat was set within the row of Victorian buildings that made up part of the façade of Lord Street. The shops beneath were protected by a wrought iron glazed canopy that might encourage estate agents to term the street as a Victorian canopied boulevard. She reflected momentarily and wondered if the canopy's original design was to keep the gentry free from aerial bombardment, whether that be from the rain or the bird droppings. However, the street was now only a shadow of its former self, as much of the grandeur was lost. Many of the shops stood empty and the canopy was neglected in certain parts. The door between two shops was the clue that there were flats above. A row of four buttons was linked to an intercom.

The name Craufurd Gaskell was the first on the list. He was the man she had come to see, the landlord. She pressed the button. The speaker crackled momentarily and a voice was heard like someone clearing their throat.

'Mr Gaskell, It's DC Lucy Teraoka. We have an appointment.'

The lock mechanism clicked and the door sprung open an inch or two.

'Come up. Top floor.'

Lucy was amazed at the length of the passageway. There were no doors to either side, only the stairs situated at the far end. At each floor level the flight turned through one hundred and eighty degrees after staging at a landing. A numbered door was to the right and a patterned Victorian leaded window ran from the ceiling to a metre from the floor. On the upper landing Gaskell was waiting.

'One gets used to the climb, DC Teraoka. Lovely name by the way.'

'And yours. Never come across that Christian name before. It's unusual.'

'It was the middle name of a famous racing driver my father was fond of and saw race on one occasion. The greatest driver never to be a world champion. Sir Stirling Moss, sadly now no longer with us but remembered by many and how will I ever be able to forget him? My father, as you can guess, was a petrolhead.' He pointed to the open door. 'It's worth the climb to be away from street level, particularly on a Friday and Saturday night, especially in the summer months. We have a number of boy racers who treat the street as a track. Come in. How may I help?'

The room was elegant. The ceilings were high and edged

by a cornice made up of an intricate plaster frieze. The room could be classed as minimalist. Dark leather chairs were carefully positioned giving a casual yet precise order. Even the wooden floorboards were painted a delicate shade of light grey. Colour was added to the white walls by the large unframed abstract canvases hanging on each. There were no curtains nor blinds covering the windows. It was stunning.

'I do hope it's not too rude to mention but you have a fabulous room,' Lucy offered.

'Not at all, it's what I do, it's my job. I've always enjoyed designing interiors. I worked on all of these four apartments. Each is very different. May I offer you coffee?' He moved towards the door to the far side of the room.

'Thank you, but no. Carla Sharpe and Callum Smith. They rented one of these for quite some time?'

He returned and sat opposite.

'Indeed. They took a three-year lease on number two but unfortunately things didn't work out. They were nice enough people and I had few issues during their tenancy. However, we had to cut short the contract owing to their personal circumstances.'

'Splitting up?'

Craufurd Gaskell smiled, the sort of smile that was a cross between trying to convey the circumstances were acceptable, and anger. The facial expression appeared quickly but took a little longer to dissipate.

'You mentioned the word "few". Anything we should know about?'

Standing, he went over to the windows that seemed to fill the wall. He looked out along Southport's main thorough-fare. 'I had a number of complaints from another tenant, regarding noise. Their parties could get a little, to put it diplomatically, on the loud side, and although they didn't break their agreement, let's say they sailed very close to the wind. The consolation with apartments of this age is that they were built well and it takes a lot for sound to travel from one apartment to another. When my father converted them, he used the best sound deadening materials available at that time and so they have additional insulation. But, they were very contrite, and sent flowers and an apology to the neighbour. The problems that came later were the rows.' He turned back to look directly at Lucy. 'He would kick her out, hide her key and refuse her entry. It wasn't frequent but often enough. If it were my partner, they'd only do it the once.'

He moved away from the window and stood facing her.

'Were you aware of any violence from either?' Lucy felt a little uncomfortable as he now stood over her.

'One could never be sure. From up here I have a direct view of the area around the entry. Come.'

Lucy moved to the window. Her discomfort returned as he moved closer.

'See? I've seen her standing there in the rain or in the cold looking extremely dejected. She was a lovely girl. When things were going well, they were a lovely couple.'

'Did you help?' She moved away from the window to put space between them. She could see the immediate dilemma on his face as he appeared to bite his lower lip.

'I did, yes, I did. I went down to check if she was ok. On one occasion she appeared to have a swelling, above her right eye I think it was. She told me she'd walked into one of the street's canopy supports. Happens a lot, especially to tourists too busy looking at the shops' windows, and bang! Now, with many of the shops gone it's people staring into their mobile phones!'

'And?'

'I brought her here. She assured me that she wouldn't go directly to her flat; we'd pass it on the way up, you see. I suggested Callum might just need time. She listened to reason and so she can't have been too drunk then.'

'Did she stay long and did she give a reason for the problem?'

'An hour or so until things calmed down. On a couple of occasions, she stayed longer, but as to the length of time I couldn't be sure. It seemed little things caused the major issues, clothes left on the floor, and drink.'

'His or her drinking issue?'

'She told me it was her but then she could have been covering for him.'

'What was the state of the apartment when they left?' Lucy stood again. This would be her last question.

'It was immaculate. They paid in full, and also presented me with a case of red wine as a thank you for my being understanding about the curtailed lease. These things happen and one has to be generous. Besides, I liked them as people and as a couple. And on a mercenary level you hope that if they are treated fairly the word spreads.'

'Neither wanted to stay as a single occupant?'

'I don't think they could afford it. Carla did ask but as I say, it's not cheap.'

Lucy turned to leave. 'Thank you, you've been most helpful.'

'Saying that the apartment was too expensive for single

occupancy or so we thought, someone took a short-term lease of four months immediately after they left. Knew about the flat, having attended a party there apparently.'

'Do you have a name and forwarding address?'

'I think so. Moved into a beautiful apartment in Liverpool. Art dealer. Shall I send it on or are you willing to wait? It could take a while.'

'As soon as, Mr Gaskell, thanks. I've an errand to run so I'll pop back in thirty minutes if you think that's adequate time to locate it?'

Gaskell smiled and escorted her to the door.

'Just one more thing. Are you married, Mr Gaskell?'

'I really don't think that has anything to do with the police or your enquiries. However, the answer is no if it puts your mind at rest.'

As Lucy stepped out onto Lord Street again, the gull's screams drew her attention. She checked the time and decided to call April with her findings. Considering the meticulous order of Gaskell's apartment, she did not believe he would be so disorganised as to not have that information immediately to hand. She suspected there was a reason for not divulging or retrieving it immediately.

'Thanks, Lucy, I think your suspicion is justified from what you say. Make sure you come away with it.'

April took the call as she was preparing for the interview with Smith. Skeeter had been taking notes as the phone was on speaker.

'Thanks, Lucy.'

'Another box ticked, and regarding the apartment, we can confirm this with him. Let's not mention our going to Gaskell's apartment. He might tell us but he might be unaware. We'll keep it as an ace card.'

Her phone rang again. 'Decent.' She listened, her eyes staring straight towards Skeeter as she jotted a note and pushed it to her: A BODY FOUND! She added further details.

'Close it down. I'm on my way.'

'Christ! Carla?' Skeeter prematurely pronounced as she jumped to her feet. 'You were right!'

April was already clearing her things into the top drawer. 'Rearrange the interview with Smith and meet me down-stairs. Not Carla but Cameron Jennings.' She paused allowing her colleague to wrestle with the information. 'One of Carla's listed friends.'

'Bloody hell! Will do. Downstairs.'

* * *

There was no need for the siren. The concealed blue strobes of the plain car were enough to allow them to move with greater urgency through the light traffic. Skeeter drove whilst April communicated with Control.

'Jennings's car has been found well away from the body. It's positioned in a lay-by at the end of Banks Road and Ralph's Wife's Lane. According to residents it's been there since early this morning.'

Skeeter glanced sideways momentarily, a look of confusion on her face. 'We're not going there? The body's located where exactly?'

'The end of Marshside Road and Marine Drive. Fortunately, the road has no development only a carpark and rough ground where the body was located. Someone flying a drone discovered it. He'd been flying some distance away from the carpark. On reviewing the images he'd taken it showed two people moving onto the waste ground behind the gate and crossing to a banked area. His drone was then flown out and away from the scene. In his statement he hadn't seen them whilst he was flying, something to do with the light on screen. He only noticed when he stopped to change the battery. His curiosity was spiked, he said, as he'd seen no one other than the occasional passing car. Fortunately for us, before he packed away he flew it over that area.

Curiosity. It was then he saw the figure curled on the mound. He lowered the drone and realised what he'd found. It's here.' April held up her phone. She glanced at the still image.

'What's the clarity like on the videos?' Skeeter turned onto Marshside Road and could see the police car parked across and blocking the road. She slowed.

'It's with the tech people who are trying to enhance it. Unfortunately, the drone was at about 200 feet and nearly a quarter of a mile away. It was returning when it captured the video of the two people. It was only a brief sighting too. According to his statement he was turning the machine towards his position so they were only caught for seconds. The battery had been very low and he had needed to get it back. However, the second flight shows the dead man clearly. We'll see that for ourselves shortly.'

'If you heard any noise when you thought you were in an isolated spot and about to kill someone would you not think twice?' Skeeter asked as she listened. There was a strange silence only broken by an occasional bird's call.

'The drone probably couldn't be heard either for wind, bird noise or its distance. They're not, I'm told, as noisy as you might think.'

They were directed to drive a further one hundred yards towards the junction of Marshside and Marine Drive. A number of vehicles parked along the road told the story. The carpark had been left locked as it was only due to open at 8.30am. They stood waiting to be escorted to the crime scene manager. The light breeze crept across the large expanse of land bringing with it the smell of brine.

'You can smell the sea, the ozone,' Skeeter announced. The sea could not be clearly seen, it was too far away at this part of the north-west coast. 'To think where we're standing was once the strandline and now the sea is way over there.'

A gull flying low tumbled and cried drawing Skeeter's gaze, admiration amplifying her thought. 'I could watch them for hours. That's why people flock here, I guess. It's beautiful, desolate and yet a stone's throw from Southport.'

Skeeter allowed herself a few minutes more as she scanned the horizon from left to right starting at the Southport Pier some distance away. She followed what she believed to be a line of the sea but it was difficult to tell until she stopped looking directly across the Ribble and Alt Estuaries towards Lytham. Beyond she could clearly see Blackpool's famous tower, a needle, erect along the flat western coast.

'The drone flyer must have been on the carpark or further out down that path. It goes quite some way from the road. If he were, that's why he couldn't see the activity over that banking. Flying rules suggest he would have to be a number of metres away.'

'From all accounts he was, sadly.'

'DI Decent!' A strong female voice called from the far edge of the carpark.

Skeeter and April moved quickly. They both immediately showed their ID. 'I'm Decent and this is DS Warlock.'

'No relation to Archbishop Derek?' the officer asked whilst scanning their cards, adding their names and the time to the Crime Scene Register.

'No, sorry. Wigan girl who's probably a lost cause in that department, even for someone as mighty as he.' She glanced heavenly and pulled a face.

'Body's over there within the confines of that bunding.

Looks as though he's having a nap. Never seen a corpse in such a relaxed position ... mind, not seen too many fortunately. The doctor's there now and it's with the crime scene investigators. There's no evidence of a struggle, as I said you'd have thought he was having a kip. I take it you've received details of the discovery, the drone?' She watched as both nodded in the affirmative. 'Who knows how long the corpse would have lain there had the chap with the drone not flown over the site and then checked what he'd filmed. Poor bugger, then flew it close to the ... Yes, sorry, you've seen the statement.'

Skeeter smiled but just wanted to get to the crime scene.

'It was fairly early this morning from all accounts. He said he'd arrived at about five but he couldn't be exact. Cycled, electric he told me, and he'd hidden it in the rough over on the bunding before heading out towards the sea. The wind is calm at that hour most days wherever you are and you can be assured of usually being alone. It gets busier later. Mainly runners and cyclists with possibly the odd early bird watcher. This area, particularly the area where the body was found, was used for sand extraction right up until 2011 or so, and then it had to be closed down as extraction agreements finished. The industrial scale digging of sand is the reason for the bunding and the planting along the top to blot the original machinery from the landscape. The lagoons positioned across the road were all part of the industry as can be seen from this.' She waved a piece of laminated paper but then returned it under the electronic tablet. 'The area's fenced at the front where there are two gates. The one further away is the less secure. It's to prevent unwelcome overnight stops. With those banks you couldn't see what was going on. There's a concrete run-in to each entrance. Cars parked close to the gates would only be seen from passing vehicles. Here, look.' The officer retrieved the laminated piece of paper and this time passed over what was a plan of the site. 'The body was located here where the site office once stood. It's on a small mound and marked with the red cross. The bunding is the highest point in the area and runs to either side but it's lower at the sea front because the original site was reduced and a temporary earth barrier was erected. People are free to walk the area and I believe there are plans to level all of the bunding and turn it back as it once was but I guess that's down to funding so we'll not hold our breath.'

'Thanks.' April moved closer to the crime scene, orientating the plan before turning towards the bunding to compare the site against the diagram. She swiftly assessed her position and the location of the body that had been marked as a red ink cross. The bunding, built to conceal the original working area, was like a green abscess on a sandy, brown-yellowy skin. The sea grass and the bushes planted along the uppermost ridge had been tortured into a submissive pose that clearly defined the prevailing wind.

'I can see why bird watchers use this place in winter as it offers some degree of shelter.'

Skeeter was growing restless. She needed to see the body as a black van marked Private Ambulance had stopped further along the road. She needed to go now.

'May we keep hold of this?' April called whilst holding the paper aloft.

The CSM nodded and moved towards the van, which was awaiting instruction and stationed on the outside of the nearer gate. As April and Skeeter moved through the further gate, they were welcomed by a string of step plates that had been placed in a line from the gate to the body. They pulled on nitrile gloves. A dark blue semi-circular screen protected the corpse from the open side facing west and the sea that was clearly a mile away. Any one coming from the sea side would have a view, particularly when the press arrived. They could get where sand could not and so privacy had to be maintained. It was immediately obvious to them both that someone had swept a pathway that was clearly visible in the surface next to the plates. It appeared as if someone had deliberately concealed any evidence of footprints that would have easily been made within the soft sand. Areas along it were tagged using yellow, triangular numbered markers whilst others of different colours were situated around the site of the body. CSI operatives continued to work the area and photograph the scene. The doctor moved down the slope and nodded a greeting.

Skeeter spoke first.

'Bloody stupid place to kill someone, on top of the mound. One side of this rough pyramid has a gentler slope otherwise it would be difficult to climb even for the more fleet of foot. Whatever the route chosen you're going to leave more prints here than you would if you were walking on the surface of the moon. The attempt at erasing them is as clear as a bell.'

'Maybe there's your answer. The body wouldn't be easily found up here and after a day or two of wind and rain, the prints would be gone. There's no wind on the moon, Skeeter!'

Skeeter nodded. 'True.' She crouched looking at the soles

of the dead man's shoes. 'Laces are undone on the left one. He could have had a nasty fall if he'd not been careful!' She looked at April but perceived only a slight shake of the head. Her attempt at humour was either ignored or lost. She knew which. The doctor climbed back up the slope and briefly presented his findings.

'Dead about three hours. Slice to the neck and the right side of the throat. The blade wasn't deep but it dragged, destroying a key artery. From my experience the blade used was curved and exceptionally sharp in both the driving tip and the blade's edge. Pathology will reveal more. Bled profusely where he fell on the top of this pile here. The body wasn't moved post death. According to these guys, the killer has tried to mask the lower area by moving the sand and also covered the track in and out as I'm sure you've seen.' The doctor wiped his brow. 'Strange place to kill someone and he was killed here I can assure you of that simple fact. We know there were two from the drone footage, even considering the poor quality. The CSM believes they might be able to enhance the footage back at the lab. Unfortunately comes with buying a cheap drone, he tells me. Both walked in but only one walked out and what's truly strange is there's no evidence of a fight nor a struggle. A bit like an accepted execution.'

The senior CSI approached and caught the final sentence as the doctor was collecting his belongings. He moved back down the slope.

'Not a pleasant thought, execution, but it certainly looks that way.'

The words put a chill down Skeeter's neck. It was a chilling announcement considering where they stood. It brought back images of the Aztec sacrifices but this was not Tenochtitlan and she could not see the stone table on which the person was sacrificed. She could, however, see a similarity considering the mound on which they stood and the body before them. April seemed to just move on. Maybe she was right.

'I don't suppose the poor drone pilot expected to be involved in something like this. What do we have from the parking area to the front? I'm sure they didn't walk here from Southport,' April mused whilst pointing in the direction of the two gates.

'It's been checked. There are a number of tyre tread patterns visible along the periphery of those gate areas and they've been photographed. We can 3-D image them later and give you the feedback. The man's wallet was checked and his identity confirmed from the image on his driver's licence. You obviously hold those details. If you're happy we need to get the body away. We're nearly done here.' He looked at both police officers optimistically.

'Did you find his phone?' April asked, already anticipating the response.

'Nothing other than the wallet and a set of keys, clearly for his car and home – sorry, one other thing, his cap.' He pointed to the base of the hill seaward. 'Probably tumbled there when he fell. We'll confirm that it's his within our report.'

'Thanks very much. There's nothing else.' April moved back along the step plates and watched as the ambulance moved onto the site.

They pulled off their gloves and stuffed them into a

yellow clinical waste bag near the rear of one of the CSI vans.

'We've been expecting to find Carla Sharpe's body for the last couple of days and now we have Cameron Jennings. So, where the hell is our Carla? You don't think, Skeeter, she could be the other person who was seen here, do you?'

'Promise of sex on the beach, a quick shag and then ...' Skeeter responded with little conviction.

'It's happened before. We need to get the footage analysed and then we can say for definite.'

Skeeter asked the CSI if she could cross the area and stand on the highest part of the bunding. He consented. She left April to study the plan and make the necessary mental adjustments to ensure its accuracy. She then shot a short video of the area marking her position with an indentation on the map's laminate cover.

The majority of the higher levels comprised rough sand and broken shells, the discarded material from the sand extraction; a sieving and washing process. Along the length, rain water had weathered cracks and formed deep ravines that followed no particular pattern. From this vantage point she could see the screen and the off-white coated figures milling around the mound. The bagged corpse was being lowered down the banking secured to a stretcher. It was when photographing the area that she spotted the one piece of natural colour growing within the whole desolate area. A solitary poppy swayed gently from the rough ground. The poignant meaning struck home hard. She had to check if it had been growing there naturally or if it had been recently planted. It had obviously grown there but she still photographed it.

CHAPTER 9

The plan April had received in the morning at the disused sand extraction site had been amended and added to the white board in the Incident Room that had quickly been established during the morning. Key links were added to the various boards. Now classed as a major crime, the missing person investigation would be stepped up rigorously within the enquiry but it was now secondary to the main line of investigation. April was now SIO of a potential double murder case, and with it came the resources and the responsibility. She looked at the photographs of both Carla Sharpe and Cameron Jennings. They stared back as if waiting for answers.

The keys found on Jennings had been for his home and his car. The car was now with CSI and the flat was in the process of being inspected by Forensics. DC Kasum Kapoor had been drafted to support the case and attached the latest findings on the murder from pathology. The CSI had been correct in his assumption. The murder weapon was described as a professional carpet fitters' blade, long and concave with a sharp curved tip. The killer knew just where to insert and drag the blade along the victim's neck. In this case, such force had been applied that it not only severed the external jugular vein but also the sternocleidomastoid muscle. It had then sliced but did not sever the common carotid artery and the internal jugular vein.

It was clear from the report that Jennings had been in a rush, as he had put on his sweater inside out. This could happen to anyone who was either frightened for themselves or for others. His phone record indicated that he had received an early call from Carla Sharpe's phone. It could be surmised that he was heading out to see her. What was not clear to the Forensic Team was the condition of his shoes. They were new. One was not properly tied whilst the other was slightly downtrodden at the back. This would have made both driving and walking especially difficult and uncomfortable, considering the slope leading to the spot where he was found. Neither did they contain any trace of the ground from that immediate area. What was found were clear traces of a loamy soil contaminated with elements of clay. This, according to their records, was compatible with and therefore more likely to be found on the farmland of the Lancashire Plain. The cap contained his DNA.

April and Tony looked through the findings.

'We need to move Carla Sharpe's missing person status up to high risk level. Like Jennings, I want access to her phone as I need live site data. Get the phone *pinged* so we know if or when it's used. We need to locate where it is and hopefully, we'll know where she is.'

Tony put in the call to gain the necessary clearance.

'Skeeter spotted the lace on one shoe when we were there

and suggested he could have been meeting with Carla for a *quick shag?'*

Tony had been looking down at his own shoes and had just started to rub the right one on the back of his trouser leg. On hearing his boss utter the word 'shag', he stopped abruptly and embarrassingly felt his face flush a little.

'Had she phoned him to tempt him there, to lure him to this remote spot at an ungodly hour with the promise of sex?'

'The police files are littered with such rendezvous with similar conclusions but why meet in one remote spot? They both have apartments, they're both single and have warm beds. Why would they go there? The place where his car was abandoned is an area full of hidden footpaths, bushes and trees suitable for alfresco sex. Why then drive to a more remote spot a mile or so away? What was their *raison d'être*? Why drive another mile or so? If we knew that we'd be closer to knowing the killer.'

April looked at Tony for a moment. He talked a lot of sense for someone who, from their general appearance, looked to be clueless. She felt sure it was a deliberate ploy. He stood looking at the board chewing some skin on his thumb. *There was more to this book than what you saw on the cover,* she thought.

'Indeed, Tony. How right you are. Forensics will be completing a full test on the shoes. If they're not his, then there should be DNA everywhere but then, as they have already stated, they were new. You'll find his shoes were changed post death. The pathologist should be able to track that. It's my understanding shoes tend to leave marks on the skin, particularly if they are tight.'

Wiping his finger on his sleeve, he turned to April.

'But if they were swapped immediately, wouldn't that …' He did not finish his question as self-doubt suddenly crept in. 'I'll just wait and see what results come back.'

April changed tack.

'According to the log we've just received, only one call was made on his phone from Sharpe since she went missing and that was early this morning. There have been no other calls made from it. So, if Sharpe is still alive, we can suspect that this was a honey trap, but if she's not, then we have a potential serial killer working in the area. The phone call was made close to the spot where his car was found. Without our insomniac drone pilot, we'd just have had another missing person.' She stopped and turned to look at Carla Sharpe's photograph.

The pause allowed Tony to carry on remedying the lack of lustre on his shoes and he began to polish the left one. 'So, you think Sharpe's already dead but just not been discovered, ma'am?' Checking the result of his swift rubbing brought a slight smile of satisfaction.

'Time will tell.' April looked down at his shoes. 'You'd be better with Kiwi and brushes but I guess you know that already.'

* * *

On returning to the station, Lucy had tracked the possible new address of the short-term tenant who had taken over the apartment after Carla and Callum Smith vacated it. There had been no forwarding address but support officers had managed to identify two people by the names Gaskell had provided. At this stage it was a case of making a sensible guess. The mobile number also given had long since been inoperative. She had the name Simon Taylor. One was now resident in Liverpool city centre, the other lived in York. For the moment, adding the name and both addresses to the board containing Sharpe's photograph was all she could do until she checked out the Liverpool address. Strangely both men were the same age but according to passport and DVLA records, were very dissimilar. From Gaskell's brief description, it seemed likely that the Simon Taylor she was seeking now lived in the centre of Liverpool. She would run further background checks before making either appointment, as she always believed being fore-warned is to be forearmed.

Callum Smith had arrived for interview twenty minutes early and was ushered to the area normally reserved for visiting solicitors. He had refused coffee and simply waved an oversized bottle of Evian at the welcoming officer before expanding on his health regime.

Skeeter and April had both received the call at the same time to inform them Smith was early. They met in the corridor on the way down and April passed her a pre-prepared interview agenda. Addenda had been added as the latest information had filtered through and both were aware the information they had could still change.

'Wicca!' a voice from an open door called out, closely followed by Fred's face. 'Just received some dashcam footage of the area in which Carla Sharpe was last seen. They'd seen the post we'd placed on the website ... proves someone's looking! The date and time fit.'

Skeeter glanced at April as they both moved swiftly into the room and peered directly at the computer screen. The image had been paused. Fred moved the cursor onto the triangle and tapped the mouse.

'As you can see the driver of this delivery van has turned off Cambridge Road and onto Hesketh Road. You'll notice there's some traffic but it's light. Now we're on Argyle Road before turning right onto Park Road.' He paused the video. 'What occurs next happens very quickly so for the guy to spot it and react is amazing. For that reason, I'll run it in slow motion. In the distance you'll see a car pull across as if going to the golf club. If you look carefully, you'll also see a runner approaching the turn in. There are a number of cars parked along the road side but you can still see the jogger's head. Watch the car and the driver.'

Fred started the video and all eyes were focused on the screen. It happened just as he had described.

'The runner hardly comes into view,' Skeeter announced as Fred brought the video back to the critical moment before letting it run again at half speed. 'Did I see the driver climb out of the car and then stand and wave?'

'You certainly saw them put their hand up,' Fred agreed. 'Whether they were waving at the person or signalling for them to stop is debatable. The person's gender cannot be ascertained from this either.'

'So, we can't confirm this was Carla Sharpe?' Skeeter turned to Fred, a clear frown spreading across her face.

Fred shook his head. 'We have a partial number plate, however, and a model but that's it.'

'Only one brake light working too,' Skeeter announced, 'so that shouldn't be too difficult to trace.'

Fred and Skeeter checked the screen again and for a brief moment it was clear that only one light was working.

'Bloody hell, Wicca, you've got eyes like a shithouse rat.' Fred chuckled and patted her shoulder.

'It's only a brief flash but it's undeniable.'

'I've already got a call out to records with make, colour and reg so once they've traced those, locating the actual car should be straightforward, providing the car hasn't had the bulb replaced in the meantime. I'll keep you posted.'

'If that were Sharpe, she was running anti-clockwise round her regular route.'

'Does it make a difference which way she runs?' April questioned.

'Some runners feel comfortable turning one way. For me it's left and so if I run a route I keep turning left until I get back. There might be the odd right turn but they would be few and far between. Which way was she running on the first video capture we got from the Park and Ride site?'

On leaving the room, April called Fred's name, being immediately rewarded by a smiling face further down the corridor. 'Check the first CCTV footage to see the direction in which she was running. If it's the same fine but if not ...' She thrust a thumb up in the air in thanks.

* * *

Smith was waiting in an Interview Room when they arrived and surprised them both by rising on their entry. He apologised for being early but a client had cancelled and he hoped the sooner the interview started the sooner he could be back at the gym.

'We'll hopefully not detain you for too long, Mr Smith.' Skeeter deliberately slotted in the word 'detain' to see if it had any effect on his demeanour. It did not. 'Please sit. My name is DS Warlock, thank you for coming in. This is DI Decent. This interview will be recorded.' She pointed to the smoked-glass dome in the ceiling corners. 'That's for your benefit and safety as much as ours. Data protection is observed and details are in the booklet in front of you.'

'Fine, fine! Is there any news on Carla?' There was anxiety in his voice.

After confirming his age and address, Smith spoke freely about their relationship and their troubles, admitting that Carla had put up with a lot from him over their period together.

'Temptation comes my way far too frequently in my job, probably the proximity and intensity in which I work. Dance instructors have a similar problem, I think.' He looked down at his hands before proclaiming, 'The type of young women I coach and my inability to say no is the biggest problem. I talked it over with Carla on many occasions. She'd been such a rock during that time. What's the song say "You don't know what you've got till it's gone"?'

'"Eaten bread is soon forgotten", my old Dad always used to say, Mr Smith,' Skeeter replied sarcastically, the disdain clearly audible in her tone.

As a result, there was a brief moment of silence as Smith looked down at his clenched hands.

'What about her drinking? Is that just her or is it because

she found it hard living in an unpredictable relationship?' April enquired whilst leaning back.

'It's been a problem ever since I've known her. Fit as a flea but can she shove it away when we're out! Can drink until she falls over. Never suffers from a hangover, see. That makes a massive difference. Me? I lose two days if I drink heavily. She can go from comatose in the evening to bright as a button and training within six hours. Used to piss me off no end I can tell you. Wasn't natural.'

'Did she have affairs?' Skeeter asked, her voice quiet. Her eyes remained on the paper in front of her as if she had the answer there and was waiting for him to either confirm it or make a mistake.

'Not that I'm aware of but who knows, other than Carla?'

'The other guilty party I would assume, Mr Smith.' She brought her eyes to meet his but he quickly looked away, either through guilt or embarrassment about which eye to focus on. 'We heard that when you were living at the flat on Lord Street you did on occasion lock her out. Tell us about this.'

'Fucking Gaskell!'

From being totally calm, even having just been admonished, he turned immediately, his anger clear in his venomous tone.

'The word is "occasionally". She'd start getting angry, querying where I'd been and it would escalate. She'd become violent, throw things, break stuff, so I'd open the door and carry her out. She was usually drunk, very drunk.'

'And you put her out on the street in that condition?'

'She was no weak female when she was like that. I'd defy any man to approach her with the wrong intention as they'd receive more than they'd bargained for believe me. I knew her.'

'Interesting wording. "Was", "knew" – past tense, Mr Smith. I'd say, "is" and "know" unless I knew something others didn't. Funny that. I'll just make a note.'

'Was, is. It's the same.' Smith took a swig from the bottle.

'Did you ever hit her?' It was April who continued the interview. As one officer stopped the other started, each voice carrying a different tone to raise or lower the intensity of the questioning. It was as they had planned.

The next silence was prolonged. 'Yes, or a simple no is all we ask at this stage.'

'Possibly.'

'What? You possibly did or you possibly didn't? Which is it? Yes or no, Mr Smith?'

'Yes. I think she riled me to get me in an angry state so that I'd lash out. She'd then demand sex. Often she'd start removing her clothing … my anger kind of turned her on.'

'When you put her out, she wasn't in your words, "turned on" then I'm guessing?'

Smith remained silent for a moment. He shrugged his shoulders as if unable to answer accurately.

'How long did you wait before you let her return?'

'It varied. Gaskell, the landlord, used to let her in. She'd go to his place and then come home. I'd get a knock and an apology.'

'So, how long would she be with Gaskell?'

'An hour or so but sometimes she'd be there all night.'

Skeeter looked at April. 'So, you're stating that you were happy that your drunken partner who might or might not be "turned on" was being entertained in a neighbour's flat all night – all night, Mr Smith?'

'He was looking after her not entertaining her. You make it sound so sordid,' Smith protested and for the second time they saw his anger escalate as he clenched his fists.

'Did she ever have sexual relations with Gaskell?' Skeeter leaned forward.

'How the hell do I know?'

'Intuition, sixth sense, uncertainty, possibility, likelihood. She was drunk, probably angry with you, undoubtedly "turned on" and wanting to get back at you. You believed that was her intention. When you parted you eventually realised how attractive a woman you had let go. You heard about or saw her with other men. You were jealous then but did the jealousy turn to rage? We can see now from our chat that you can quickly become angry. Did your anger culminate in violence as it has in the past?'

Skeeter glanced at April as if inviting her to pick up the baton. The tension was now palpable. The smile had been replaced with a scowl and his whole body had stiffened. Veins were clearly visible to either side of his neck and his temples. His face was flushed.

'Are you blaming me for her disappearance? Are you seriously accusing me of killing her?'

'Nobody has mentioned anyone being killed, Mr Smith, other than you.'

It was now open for Skeeter. 'Did you put her out again – permanently this time because you realised that you'd lost her and she was getting along just fine without you? New flat, new men in her life, yes, plural and of course her friends. She didn't need you and she would no longer come running home?' Skeeter's question was direct and purposefully designed to rile.

'No! Utter rubbish. We'd finished. I didn't see her for ages before she went missing. I told the officer that the first time I was interviewed. You'll have it in your records.'

Skeeter opened the file and slid a still photograph of him standing in the shop. 'You're with Carla there. Is that you and is that Carla?'

He looked at the photograph but did not pick it up. He then nodded.

'We need you to speak as gestures can be misconstrued on film.'

'Yes.'

'Yes, we have your initial statement which now seems to be contradicted by that evidence. You told us a lie, an untruth. Why was that, Mr Smith? What exactly are you hiding?'

CHAPTER 10

On hearing the news on Cameron Jennings's murder, following so quickly after Carla's disappearance, Stuart Groves felt disquieted. The details were here in black and white. He had taken the *Liverpool Echo* from the newspaper rack and his friend's face had stared back. That face was the same face that had been here, in the café not long ago, arguing about whose turn it was to pay. 'When in life does the average man personally know anyone who's been murdered?' he mumbled to himself, loudly enough for a woman on the next table to look his way, frown, before moving her chair a little further away. Not many people ever do fortunately and here he was, within a matter of a few days, finding he had one friend missing and another murdered. He immediately felt as though the sword of Damocles was hanging above his head.

He did not look to check, instead he looked out of the café window at the light drizzle flushing Lord Street. He thought about Cameron and a simple question looped in his mind: why him? Turning back to the report brought even more confusion. For one thing, Cameron was never an early bird so to be murdered at that time in the morning was absurd. The place seemed to make no sense either. Yes, he was a runner so he might be out along Marine Drive. But, was he out running? He ran later in the morning usually. He looked at the photograph of the shoes featured in the article, clearly identified as evidence. He never wore that type of footwear and he certainly never ran in brogues not even for a bus. He felt a strange tumbling within his stomach and made a dash for the toilet.

* * *

Lucy and Tony Price pulled off Strand Street and into the underground parking area for Liverpool One, the large conglomerate comprising shopping centre, leisure facilities and accommodation. The specified parking area was on the first level. It had to be said that neither found the apartment block inspiring as it seemed to be constructed mainly from glass. Interestingly, it was within a hundred yards of the Merseyside Police HQ.

The entrance hall to the apartments was airy and contemporary. To the right was an area holding elegantly designed post boxes, row upon row, each numbered. Two dark grey leather settees were positioned next to the concierge's desk. He had watched with interest as they emerged from the carpark elevator.

Tony nodded before walking to the bank of ten buttons under the label 'Floor Eleven'. He pressed button four.

'Taylor,' the voice announced with unusual clarity for an intercom.

'Mr Taylor, you're expecting us at two.'

The lock on the door clicked and swung slightly. 'Just take either lift.'

'Hold the door, sir. Your car registration, if I may. We don't want to find it clamped on our return, do we now?' The concierge smiled, a smile that could curdle milk but was well intended. Tony looked at Lucy in the hope she would know. She checked the key fob and read it out. 'Thank you. Your first time here I see.' With that he returned to his seat and continued to monitor the three large CCTV screens.

Arriving on the eleventh floor had been less of a challenge than they had thought and apartment 114 would have been clearly visible even without Simon Taylor standing outside the door.

Once inside the apartment Tony could not contain his enthusiasm for the view from the expanse of glass that seemed to fill the far wall. A small balcony ran along its full length. Tony whistled low and slow as he moved closer, his admiration made very apparent.

'Sir, that is some view. May I?'

'Please, allow me.'

Taylor slid open the door and Tony walked outside. The whole of the riverfront was laid before them stretching from the Albert Dock along to the Three Graces and then beyond. The view the apartment captured was that of the iconic Liverpool waterfront and the UNESCO World Heritage site for which it is famous.

'I bet it's a special view in all weathers and at night, Mr Taylor. I've seen it from our police building further down the road but the balcony makes all the difference.'

'On a clear evening it is truly special, when the sun has set and Mother Nature's illuminations blend with the complementing lights of the waterfront. Yes, it's stupendous. The real beauty is in the subtle daily change of the light and how that plays on the colour of the river. It's loving art that makes me see these things – an artist's eye you might say. Sorry! I'm being rude. May I offer you tea or coffee?'

'Thanks, but no. We just need to chat about your time in Craufurd Gaskell's flat,' Lucy answered, eager to proceed.

Tony had moved inside and taken a seat next to Lucy.

'Craufurd, yes. I was there for a short time. I had a contract for four months although I didn't stay the full term but I paid up fully. It was when I was waiting for this to become available. City living suits me and my business but I'd seen the Southport apartment having attended a party there and liked the whole ambience of the space and its general position. Being close to the Atkinson Gallery was a key consideration. So, for short term it suited me. It became available at the right time you could say.'

'You knew both previous tenants then?'

'Initially, no. Strange circumstances how I met Carla, yes, Carla Sharpe and her partner was I think, Colin Smith?' he hesitated.

'Callum Smith,' Lucy corrected.

'Sorry, you're right, of course. Callum. Bonny fellow. As I was saying, I was staying in a hotel and one evening I saw Carla sitting on a bench on Lord Street. She looked a little worse for wear shall we say, so I asked if all was well. She said she was taking the air. She pointed to her flat. Anyway, we just started to chat for maybe five or ten minutes and then she walked across the road. Within minutes she'd gone in and I thought no more about it until I saw her with friends in a pub a couple of nights later. A Friday, I believe it was. Surprisingly, she'd recognised me sitting on my own and came over with a bottle of wine, she said it was for my kindness. It was sweet of her even to remember me. It was then she invited me to a party later. I accepted.'

'How many times did you go to the apartment?'

'Two, maybe three at most.'

'Did you meet either Callum or Carla socially outside their home?'

'I bumped into Carla at a restaurant in Formby, *The Bistro*. I'd gone with a friend for lunch and she was there with Craufurd. I had to look twice but I was sure it was her. I didn't go over. Well, you just don't know the circumstances do you?'

'Do you know when this was?'

Taylor picked up his phone and checked the diary. 'Yes, the 15th of last month. That's a Thursday, I believe. Yes.'

'Have you seen her since, or either Callum or Craufurd?'

'I called in to see Craufurd only last week about some paintings he needed for a commission on which he was working. You're aware that I buy and sell art works for a living? Craufurd is an interior designer and since meeting we have worked on a couple of projects together. We communicate mainly over the ether, the internet rather than meeting in person, that way you save so much time. He shows me the space he's trying to fill and I send him the images of the art works I know to be available.'

'Did you know about Carla going missing?'

'I did, it's been on the news and Craufurd telephoned to let me know. As I've said, I barely knew the woman but it's still extremely distressing considering the circumstances.'

Tony slipped a photograph of Jennings onto the table in front of Taylor. 'Have you seen this man before, Mr Taylor?'

Taylor stood, collected a copy of the local paper and placed it in front of Tony. 'Snap. Funny isn't it. We have a Carla, a Craufurd, a Callum and a Cameron. Thank goodness I don't have a 'C' at the start of my names.'

'Let me rephrase that. Have you met Jennings?'

'In all honesty, I couldn't say. I don't know him personally and he's neither within nor on the periphery of my friends. I don't like the term "inner circle", it's the dubious connotations.' He tapped the frontpage headline. 'But reading that, nor is he likely to be.'

The interview was winding to a close, and Lucy and Tony stood before thanking Taylor for his help. Tony took a last look from the window.

'Great that. Stunning!' his accent suddenly seemed even stronger.

Neither Tony nor Lucy spoke as the escalator dropped them in the lobby. The head of the concierge popped over the screen but quickly returned as if he were expecting a single round from some hidden sniper to come his way. Within minutes they were driving past the Liver Building.

'Your thoughts, Tony?'

'Beautiful flat.'

Lucy shook her head and sighed. It could wait.

CHAPTER 11

It was a curious sight as more birds fought to be near the head of the scarecrow than the farmer had ever seen. Even though he was positioned some distance away both the noise of the birds' calls and the frantic flapping could be heard within the tractor's cab. It was mainly the gulls along with some rooks or were they crows? He could never differentiate even after living a rural life since childhood. He found identifying those birds within the Corvid family difficult unless it was a magpie or jay. Those he definitely knew. Within the frantic confusion, their screams were both piercing and eager. Having been distracted long enough, his curiosity got the better of him and he turned off the engine and climbed down from the cab. Trudging towards the field containing the scarecrow, he collected a stick from the hedge. *Should have made a bloody scaregull if that's what these noisy blighters are.* He checked the polythene laid on the earth as mulch to keep the soil warm and stop evaporation of the moisture. It rippled serpent-like in the light breeze, but was held firm by the number of soil bags placed around the edge. The condensation clearly clouded the inner surface.

It was the smell that first hit him, not the smell of freshly turned earth that had filled his nostrils this past hour but the distinctive smell of something dead. It slapped him when it penetrated his nostrils and there it lingered. Pausing, he looked across the field's corrugated surface. He had often found the odd fox or deer that had been clipped on the main road by a passing vehicle. The animal usually managed to limp away only to die a few hundred metres from the road, but as far as he could see there was nothing.

Approaching the standing figure, he started to swing the stick in a circle above his head, calling out to disperse the birds, making them take flight before they returned their own call of annoyance at being disturbed. The flash of black-blue wings, an almost iridescent sheen blazed a contrast against white-grey clouds. The gulls' brazenness and screaming took more effort to disperse. Many of the birds settled in the trees and along the far hedge, some fifty metres away. Those birds brave enough remained close. The air grew still apart from the occasional disgruntled bird call and a light buzz. The farmer scanned in the direction of the sound but could see nothing. Placing a finger in his ear, he waggled it before listening again. It had gone. 'Bloody ear wax,' he muttered turning his gaze back to the scarecrow.

The smell became a stench, a pungent mix not dissimilar from a cocktail of bad eggs and rotten cabbage. It was then that he noticed the differences in the scarecrow. After all, he had made the thing and put it there a couple of weeks before, as he had done each year. That was not the jacket nor the trousers. Although they were similar in type, they were clearly not those in which he had dressed the mannequin. He paused as a flush of uncertainty rose from his stomach spawned by the smell that seemed to vanish momentarily. The head on his scarecrow would never flop, it was fixed to the torso. He noticed that the body had sagged too as if the whole thing had been crucified and the arms and shoulders were carrying the full weight. The mannequin weighed little.

Removing his handkerchief, he held it to his nose and mouth before venturing closer. Rounding the end of a hedge, it was there he located the source of the smell, the rotting remains of what could be seen to be a young deer. Moving round its semi-buried carcass he walked further to stand facing the scarecrow. It took a few moments before realising at what he was looking. It was definitely human and it was definitely dead. The smell, now carried away from him on the light breeze. He lowered his handkerchief. The CDs swivelling from the ends of the sleeves and between the legs, catching and flashing the reflected light, seemed to be the only living things. The cap was on the floor and the woman's hair seemed matted to her skull. The goggles hung from one side exposing the face, a face that had been the centre of the pecking and feeding frenzy. What they had taken in one end they had released from the other; bird droppings littered the head and shoulders.

It took a minute before he added to the scene by vomiting across the faint shadow that ran to his feet. Wiping his mouth, he tossed away the handkerchief before fumbling in his pocket for his phone only to realise that he had left it in the tractor. Slipping and stumbling, he ran as best he could. The stick was now forgotten.

Nearly a mile away, captured images of the fleeing

farmer, the spectre at the feast, and the returning birds could be clearly seen. Had he heard the drone? Had he seen it? Shakily, his finger found the button on the control that stopped recording before bringing the drone back. From three hundred and five feet in the air and keeping station downwind of the activity it had, he had hoped, remained unobserved and unheard. Within minutes the drone's legs were folded and the gimbal protected. He would, however, wait. His curiosity had been piqued to see if and when the activity around the scarecrow intensified.

The birds quickly returned. The first to arrive found the warm vomit more attractive than the corpse and another squabble soon erupted bringing with it the calling and flapping. It did, however, bring an extended respite for Carla whose faceless head lolled and her hair waved as if in silent protest.

It took less than fifteen minutes for the first responders to arrive at the farmyard, a fast-track paramedic and a local police patrol.

Stuart Groves had regained most of his composure and after careful consideration checked the contacts on his phone. He could not help but look at those for Carla and Cameron. His stomach churned briefly before he quickly flicked through stopping at Bill Rodgers. He tapped the number but received his answerphone.

'Bill, it's Stu. Call me when you can. Cheers.'

* * *

The Interview Room seemed to become more and more claustrophobic the more pressing the questions. Callum Smith continued to protest his innocence.

'I went to apologise. See if we could move forward, and if not be lovers, then remain good friends.'

'And that's why in the week running up to her disappearance you were in this CCTV footage, you were at the salon?' Skeeter asked.

'I received a message from Carlos, the lad who works with her, his real name's Brian, I believe. He messaged and then called me and said that Carla was always still mentioning my name and asking if she'd done the right thing by leaving me. He said he thought she still loved me. He was very close to her, idolised her and that's why …'

'Yes, we know.'

'Well, I just wanted to find out if it were true. I was going to ask her to come back in some way. I realised what type of person I'd let go.'

'Did she ever spend time at your new place?'

Smith shook his head. 'No and I never went to hers. When I see her in here,' he pointed to his head, 'she's always in the old apartment, where I knew her and where we lived.'

He pushed the photograph back across the table. 'I honestly don't know where she is. Do you think she's safe?'

Skeeter collected the information she had spread on the table together, tapped it before sliding it into the folder. 'As you know her better than anyone, only you can answer that. We on the other hand can only hope, pray and do our best to locate her. Thank you for your time. We will be in touch.' She emphasised the word *will*, letting her eyes focus on his.

He stood, thanked them and left.

As April and Skeeter moved along the corridor after showing Smith to the reception area, the officer moved out to the front counter and approached April.

'Message for you. I was about to interrupt your meeting. Urgent, ma'am.' He nodded at Skeeter before returning behind the glass screen.

She read it. 'Shit! They've found a body and they believe it's Carla Sharpe. We're meeting Mason there and he specifically requests your attendance, Wicca.'

'Joy!' Skeeter pulled a false smile. 'He must really like me!'

CHAPTER 12

The whole of Midge Mill Lane was closed off by police cars and tape; a flapping plethora of blue-and-white plastic strips announced it was the boundary of a crime scene. It oscillated further when April's car arrived. Looking at the map, it showed a narrow lane, about two miles in length. It had been bypassed years ago relieving it of traffic and noise, but instead bestowing it with pot holes as it was now seemingly forgotten. Today, ironically, it had taken a death to bring it back to life.

They observed the usual procedures until directed to park in Mill Farm's yard. The remains of the windmill stood on the smallest of hills that was a high point for the flat surrounding farm land. Two CSI vans were parked further along the lane.

Skeeter climbed out and immediately scanned the area. To the west the land was flat and endless. It was not to her liking. *Flat as a witch's tit,* she thought, bringing a smile to her lips as she turned her gaze east where the ground was on the rise. A large copse of trees swung over the hill before breaking into the hedgerows as if compensating for the bland landscape opposite. North and south seemed to be a mixture of both and to her that was what farmland should look like. Tan Pit Cottage, her home, was within the folds of similar hills, probably the highest point once you move away from the coast before you strike the Pennines proper.

DCI Mason walked across the yard wearing green wellington boots. They looked incongruous with the suit as the trousers appeared ruched.

'This way, farmer seems fine, more worried about birds pecking his spring cabbage to be honest with you. Once he'd got over the initial shock and had a brew, he wanted to continue working on the field below the crime scene. Time's money, he persistently advises.' He paused resting his hands on his hips. 'He makes the scarecrows in the first place so to find one had been exchanged for a corpse. Apparently these scarecrows have been renowned in the area for some time.' He handed April an electronic tablet. 'That's the image of the scarecrow and whoever did this copied the original well. If you flick along you can see the corpse. Almost bang on for detail. Slight difference in jacket but to anyone passing along the road it would appear the same. Even he didn't notice until the birds started their feeding frenzy, and he made the bloody thing. If you get a whiff of death, the farmer found and moved the rotting carcass of a deer near the hedge there. May have encouraged the feeding frenzy.'

* * *

The drone sat in his hand like a miniature dog, legs outstretched. He wiped the camera and the gimbal moved loosely. The small, green light flashed at the back of the body, a signal that it was connected to the controller. Finding a flat area, he placed the drone down carefully and collected the handset. It was ready to fly. Seventeen satellites had linked with it and the craft knew its home point. He tapped the take-off button on the screen and a circle appeared in the centre. Resting his finger on it the green line illuminated as it ran around the circle. On completing three hundred and sixty degrees, he lifted his finger. The drone rose a metre into the air. Within two minutes it hovered at three hundred and five feet, its eight blades barely audible. Turning the drone towards the farm, he pushed the right lever forward and the craft began its journey, unseen and unheard.

* * *

The scene, where white suited figures were walking around the blue and white forensic tent concealing the body, seemed surreal, almost unworldly. The alien forms, the mono-coloured ground, and the polytunnels in the distance all contrived to make Skeeter imagine she was witnessing man's early colonisation of a planet. Even the colour of the contin-uous blanket of cloud and the lack of breeze enhanced her perception.

Looking down at the tablet's screen, she scrolled through the images. The footprints, pushed deep into the soil were probably those of the farmer. The close-up shots of the face were disconcerting. The plethora of beaks had torn away flesh leaving a raw, sinewy mass of marks beneath the fringe line. The eyes were long gone along with the nose. The knotted gag had forced the lips forward and had been easy picking leaving gums and teeth exposed. The area around the sliced neck had also received attention from the scavenging birds.

'Similar injury as in Jennings's murder, a ripping and tearing but here the birds have taken the injury to a higher level.'

In further photographs it was clear that the ears too had been savaged. The blood had obviously settled in the lower portion of the body leaving the exposed upper flesh ghostly and pallid.

'Copied even down to the spinning discs. Clever. Our killer didn't want this to be found for a while and we thought that too about Jennings's location. Isolated spots seem to be the name of this killer's game. My bet is that the soil on the shoes will be a perfect match to that near this body,' April announced before looking at Mason and Skeeter. 'The killer's teasing himself, or us.'

Skeeter focused on the image of the red cap; the white swoosh mark partly concealed in the loose soil. 'Or just bloody stupid and filled with an abundance of self-importance. See it all the time in bouts when visiting wrestling clubs come to take us on. The loud, arrogant ones are usually on their arses first so let's hope he goes the same way – seems a cocky bugger. What do we know about the cap?' She passed over the screen and pointed to the image of the red cap settled within the dirt next to the wellington boot, the opening facing upwards where it had fallen.

'According to the farmer that wasn't the original but the goggles were. We're uncertain as to the CDs. Originally, they were just old music CDs that were damaged but I'm assured the jacket, trousers and boots are not those clothing the original figure which was an old shop mannequin. There are similar figures dotted around the farm but this one, according to the farmer, was placed closest to the public road because it was most lifelike. They were apparently brought here when a local shop closed and they were throwing them out.'

'Prophetic,' Skeeter uttered, a degree of cynicism to her tone.

It was April who heard the faint intermittent buzzing. She paused, turning in the direction of the noise. She scanned the farmland and out towards the main road some distance away. A motorbike appeared from behind some trees which ran along the road's edge; the engine note, a growing whine, was amplified before falling away again as it disappeared from view. Silence returned. She continued to look but could observe nothing other than a few birds.

'It's amazing how sound travels out in the open. Did you hear that buzzing?' Skeeter questioned. 'The Goddess Nike ...'

April nodded but Mason shook his head in confusion.

All eyes fell on her.

'Goddess Nike. What?' Mason muttered.

'... the swoosh on the cap she was wearing. Well, if my knowledge serves me well, the winged goddess Nike flew around the battlefields honouring the victors with glory and fame. Her main attributes were victory, speed and strength.'

Mason looked across at her. 'I think Sharpe will get her fame. The press will be as eager as the gulls and the crows to get here to spread this story all over the front pages and the internet tomorrow. In place of glory, we just need to get rid of the 'l'.'

'Vultures, sir. The press was already on the outer barrier as we arrived. They smell stories like this.'

Mason laughed out loud. 'We utilise the press, don't ever forget that. Let's get on. We have the farmer's statement and once we get this body away, we can close up here. We need the post mortem results urgently as well as forensic results on the clothing and the discs. I also want a comparison on the shoe. I've a feeling most of the clothes will be from charity shops and therefore the DNA tests will be up the shoot before we begin, but we can live in hope. It's in your hands, Decent. Good call with this. Didn't go unnoticed.'

* * *

The screen images taken from the drone were as sharp as could be expected considering its height and distance from the scene. The tent and the three figures positioned some way from the main activity were visible but their faces unclear. The drone had hovered long enough and the battery was running low. With the left lever on the control panel, he turned the drone away and then pressed the button to stop recording. Within two minutes the drone was directly above its take-off point; the satellites and compass had done the job. As it came in to land, he held out an outstretched flat right hand. The drone hovered momentarily, the belly sensors keeping it away. A further press of the left lever and an automated voice from the handset speaker announced the drone was landing. Fingers wrapped the body and the rotors came to a stop. Silence reigned. Replaying the footage, the scene had a surreal appearance but even on enlarging the paused image the figures' faces were too pixilated to identify.

* * *

Bill Rodgers sat looking at Fred and Lucy. He had accepted the offer of a coffee. He ran his first finger around the lip of the mug, the motion slow and deliberate. Although Fred and Lucy had been informed of the latest development in Carla's case, it would not be mentioned. She would remain missing for the duration of this interview at least.

'It must have been a shock hearing of Cameron Jennings's death and Carla Sharpe's disappearance. I believe they were both good friends of yours?'

Rodgers continued to study the cup and his finger slowly stopped rotating. 'It was. Any news on Carla?'

'Your friendship with Carla. How long have you known her?'

'A few years. We had a fling before she met Mr Handsome, Callum Smith. It was nothing too serious.' He paused and a slight laugh caught his throat. 'Funnily enough, when they split, she rejoined our group. Good for a laugh, our Carla. Bit of a piss head though on occasion.'

'What do you know about the breakdown of her relationship with Smith?' Lucy enquired whilst flicking over the notes placed in front of her.

'It went really smoothly initially, their relationship I mean. They moved in together and all seemed well. He was a bit of a bugger with other women, his clients from what I heard. It happened a few times, but they seemed to patch it up. I only heard things about that side of it from gossip – from other friends – mutual friends.' He drained his coffee.

'I asked specifically about the breakdown of the relationship but I'm interested in what you're telling us. Go on.'

'Like I said. It was mostly heard from mutual friends. That's it really.'

'Any violence involved? Did you hear about that from these mutual friends?' Fred stood and leaned against the wall. His stance changed the dynamic of the room and he felt it gave him the high ground.

'I know she could be a bit of a spitfire when she'd had a few. I'd seen that before and after that relationship. She could goad others into starting trouble easily too. She'd be the one to strike the match and create the spark and then she'd step back and watch the fireworks.'

'You saw and experienced that?' Lucy asked, surprise on her face.

'On a couple of occasions, yes. Others in the group would try to defuse the situation, calm her down. They knew her but this was always after booze. Normally she wouldn't say boo to a goose. Butter wouldn't melt …'

'Did she encourage you to start trouble?'

Rodgers looked at them both, knowing they were aware of his past. 'On occasion but I've more control now. Older and wiser you could say.'

'Was your relationship post her breakup with Jennings platonic?' Fred's question stopped him in his tracks and his expression changed immediately. He pushed away the mug and swung back on the chair like a defiant child.

'What sort of question's that? What the hell's it got to do with you or anyone else?'

The pause was palpable as Fred returned to his seat, looking across at Rodgers and then at Lucy. 'Shall I tell him, or shall I leave it to you?' He did not wait for the reply. 'You see, Mr Rodgers. Let's imagine a scenario now. Let's imagine that Carla doesn't come home but her body is found. It doesn't matter if there are suspicious circumstances surrounding her death or not as it will be treated as a suspected murder or suicide from the off. That will mean the coroner will be involved, an autopsy, DNA. You know what DNA is? It's that magic stuff that unravels mysteries that were once unfathomable. From that we will discover many things about Carla's life, her personal life and with that, Mr Rodgers, the personal lives of others. So, ponder on that for a moment and when you've had a think, reconsider my question. And, Mr Rodgers, if the worst happens and we find a body and in or on that body is your DNA, then two plus two might make four. Answering questions now might save you an awful lot of trouble should things take a turn for the worst.'

Rodgers's attitude changed immediately as if someone had hit a switch. He swung back towards the table and grasped the mug as if it were a security blanket.

'When she split, she contacted me to go out. She asked if I'd invite her out with the friends we had. I agreed. On the first night out, she propositioned me. She suggested a one-night stand but made it clear that she was not looking for a relationship, or the responsibility a relationship brings were her words, whatever they mean. If I got the nod then happy days.'

'Did she give the nod to any others?'

'Not too sure. I would like to think not but knowing her state after the split it's more than likely. Maybe it was her way of getting back at Smith. I'm no psychologist.'

'Right! Go on.'

'As I always say, women can't live by bread alone.' He

looked directly at Lucy as if hoping for some support of his theory but received nothing in return. 'Her motto was *Life is for living – just live it!* If you've been to her flat, you'll have seen it written on one of the walls. So, for the purpose of DNA, the answer is yes on occasion and I've been to the flat and she's been to mine.'

'And the last time you had sex?'

Rodgers's answer came back immediately at full volley.

'The day before she went missing.'

'The day before? Please explain, but before you do, I'm going to caution you. This does not mean you're under arrest it means you'll be under oath and as we advised at the beginning this is recorded for your security as well as ours.'

Lucy cautioned him before she repeated the question. 'Talk us through your meeting with Carla on the day before she went missing.' She added the day and date.

'The date and the time's correct, yes. It came out of the blue, the message, that is. She'd been out for a meal with Debbie. It was simple and straightforward. She asked me to meet her at hers and bring a bottle.'

'What time did you receive it and what time did you arrive?'

He took out his phone. 'Received it at ten fifteen. She wanted me to be there after eleven fifteen. I wasn't late, let's put it that way.' He raised his eyebrows. 'So, in answer to your personal question we had sex then. It was the last time.'

'Did you stay the night?'

'No, that wasn't part of the invitation, never was. I left about two. I remember seeing the clock on the Atkinson when I walked home and it was two thirty.'

'Were you then in a relationship, Mr Rodgers?'

Fred and Lucy could see the immediate reticence flash across his face. The signals were subtle but clear enough. It was accompanied by a shuffling of his feet. He nodded.

'Does the nod of the head suggest that you were and you still are?'

'Yes, Debbie Sutch, but we don't live together or anything like that. It's just a relationship. We do our own stuff and neither of us communicates about that.'

'Right. Did you then know they were meeting that evening for a meal and that they were also meeting again for lunch the following day?'

'Lunch? No, I knew about the Italian meal but lunch, no.'

It was clear that the thought brought a degree of concern. 'Are you sure?'

'It was Ms Sutch who initially raised concerns of her going missing. Surely you were aware of that?'

'No, I bloody well wasn't.'

'When did you last meet Debbie?'

'Last week. We were supposed to go out over the weekend but she was too upset about Carla. She didn't want company. I'm supposed to be seeing her tonight.'

'Is she aware that you and Carla are still intimate?' Lucy asked as she raised her eyes to meet his.

Rodgers laughed lightly and shook his head. 'What do you think?'

'Mr Rodgers?'

'No, at least I don't think so.'

CHAPTER 13

Skeeter was the first back at her desk and she googled the goddess Nike. It was as she had described to her colleagues, her memory was sound. *Why would the killer change the cap?* she thought as she copied the logo. Adding the words that described the goddess and her actions onto a tacky note before sticking it to the side of her computer screen.

Looking through the forensic file on Jennings, she was desperate to locate a link or connection other than the possibility of a match with the soil sample found on the shoe he was wearing. 'Someone doesn't go to this trouble disposing of bodies.' She stopped talking to herself as a thought came to her. As a wrestler, Skeeter was very much aware of body weight and the need for technique to lift anyone off the floor. Since she had been old enough, she had trained with the leather wrestling dummies in the gym. They were full adult size and weight mannequins that had a certain sado-masochistic appearance and she had acquired the necessary technique. This training had taught her that to move a dead weight was very difficult. The average male could not lift a dead and flaccid body off the ground, never mind transport an adult body, without strenuous pulling and dragging. Studying the images taken at the crime scenes, neither showed signs of a struggle, nor did they appear to show that the body was dragged. To get Carla onto the cross-like frame would not have been easy without extensive disturbance of the soil around the post. Although the ground had been disturbed, it did not suggest a struggle of any kind. She brought up onto screen the photographs taken at Carla's crime scene. Pathology would identify grip and drag marks if that had been the case. She was convinced they would find none.

Tony ambled in to the room, whistling an unidentifiable tune, a can of lemonade in hand.

'Want one?' He held up the can. 'Best lemonade to whet your whistle. Have them in my desk.'

'Thanks! Love one. By the way, your whistle is sharp enough to crack glass.'

'How kind of you to say,' he mumbled as he crossed to his desk and took out another can.

'I'd also like to hear your wise words, you being a man who knows all about soil. You carry much of the stuff beneath your finger nails! My mother would say you could plant spuds under those.' She leaned from behind the screen to see a middle finger retracting.

'Ha, bloody, ha. Witch.' He threw over a can. 'Let's hope that blows your head off when you open it.'

She positioned it towards the waste bin before angling

and pulling the ring. The hiss and the sudden ejection of some of the froth hit the bin's metal side. She smiled at Tony. 'More ways of killing a pig than stuffing it full of cherries.' Taking a sip, she pointed to her screen. 'Just been to the site where Carla Sharpe's body was discovered. Look.'

She flicked through the images of her scarecrow posture as Tony watched. 'Bloody hell! We've a warped one here. How the fuck did he get her into that position?'

'That's my point. He didn't have to. Why not?'

Tony slurped the dregs from the can allowing a belch to erupt, loud and long. 'Better out than in. Let me guess. There was more than one person involved in committing this crime? Maybe Jennings was involved?'

'Nope. Let me tell you my thoughts. She walked there voluntarily. She believed that he wasn't going to kill her. Maybe something he'd said or promised. Maybe she believed it to be a hoax.'

'Hoax? Strapped to a pole in the middle of a bloody field. Fucking strange friends she must have.'

'Ever heard of sadomasochism?'

Tony frowned and Skeeter could see he had suddenly taken the thought seriously. He tossed the empty can into the bin.

'She was fully clothed from these images. Do we know if she'd been raped or subjected to some strange act of perversion? I know this shit goes on but ...'

'Not as yet. Just like Jennings went to the isolated spot voluntarily, maybe so too did Carla here. What were they promised, I wonder?' Skeeter tapped the screen.

'Have we checked the IT equipment at their homes? If

they're into this kind of stuff it should be all over their internet search history.'

'It's in hand as we speak.'

'Phone records with us yet?' Tony quizzed.

'Time, it always takes time. Had it been a child who'd gone AWOL then it would have been done within twenty-four hours but these two only reached high risk status and fast track and all that it entailed once their bodies were found.'

* * *

'May we turn our attention to Cameron Jennings now? How well did you know him?' questioned Lucy.

'We've been mates for years. Occasionally went to the football together but he sometimes worked away so we'd only get together when he returned. We'd meet up at the weekend with a group, Carla was one and Debbie.'

'Others?'

'It depended on circumstances. If it was a birthday or a beach barbecue then it could be quite a few.'

'We'll need a list of the people within this group. Those who met regularly and then we will look at your contacts more broadly. Do you have your phone with you, Mr Rodgers?'

He removed it from his pocket. Fred raised a hand and an officer appeared at the door. 'Do a phone read and extract the contacts' list, Facebook contacts and messages, usual stuff, please and then return it as soon as. Photographs too. Looking specifically around this date.' He handed him a slip of paper.

'You can't do that! Bloody hell that's my personal property. You need a warrant or something. I have rights, don't I? I want to see a solicitor and I want one before that phone leaves this room.'

'Sorry, but we don't need a warrant, and yes, you do have rights. It is a perfectly acceptable procedure and unless you've something to hide, I really can't understand your protestations. If it happened as you say it happened, Mr Rodgers, then it will be confirmed on your phone. Can we get on? Let me take you back a few years. Your criminal record. Affray. Have you reformed, Mr Rodgers?'

The red suffused Bill's face and the veins on his neck and temple began to protrude. He slipped his hands below the table, clenching them as he fought to control his growing anger. 'It was a one off.'

In contrast, Lucy's voice was calm and gentle. 'To our knowledge, sir, you've been warned on many an occasion both pre- and post-offence. Football matches seem to be the common ground but also violence much closer to home.'

'I made a mistake, I listened to gossip.'

'You caused serious injury to a person you suspected was having a relationship with your girlfriend. "Too familiar" were your words to the magistrates. "He was too familiar when I saw them together." Did you ask if he knew your girlfriend?'

Rodgers was about to speak but Fred held up his finger and he stopped.

'No. You simply beat him senseless. Did you do that to Jennings too? When you'd lured him out onto the sands where it was all quiet.' He let the question hang momentarily like a bad smell. Rodgers tried to avoid a response by turning his face away and narrowing his eyes. His breathing immediately came in short, sharp intakes as if it were a controlling exercise, a method of quelling his growing anger. 'Did she tell you she'd been shagging Jennings too and that he was better than you – bigger and better? Did you revert to your old Mr Hyde or is it Dr Jekyll? Do you know, Mr Rodgers, I can never remember who was the evil one in those two, can you? Did you kill him, Mr Rodgers? We'll also need to take a swab for DNA elimination.'

Rodgers brought his hands onto the table and placed them palms down as he turned to look Fred directly in the eye.

* * *

DC Kasum Kapoor approached Skeeter, a file in her hand. We've just received this and I heard you'd been waiting. A matter of urgency, I believe.'

'Results from the IT search?'

'Indeed, ma'am. Is there anything else?' She waited, hands folded, her back straight as Skeeter looked into the file.

'No, no that's perfect. Sorry, yes. Anything on the phones?'

'Not as yet.'

'Thank you.' She watched as Kasum moved away. 'That young lady does yoga, you can tell from her posture.' She took a side glance at Tony. 'Whereas you're a grand master of slobbery. There's a difference, it's only subtle, yes, but there's a difference.'

Tony pulled a face. 'If you bloody say so! I tell you what, she's pretty though.'

Skeeter extracted notes from the file. 'Nothing to suggest SM or the like. Some porn but nothing we should worry about. Strangely, there's more in Carla's computer history than in that of Jennings's. We also have confirmation of the material on Facebook, Twitter and other sites and their contacts. They're each on the others but we knew that from Debbie's phone. Interestingly the tech people have high-lighted certain emails for our immediate attention. Don't you just love them?'

Tony leaned over her shoulder. Her tightly plaited hair was immaculate. 'Do you do your hair yourself, Wicca?'

'The bloody list, look at the list or bugger off,' Skeeter grumbled.

'Jennings! He sent flowers to Carla.'

'What date was that?'

Tony checked. 'Just over a month ago. She was living alone then. Let's see what was written on the card if there was one: "Thanks for your understanding, x".'

'What the bloody hell does that mean? Understanding of what I wonder.' Skeeter shot back at Tony.

'Look there, we have communication between Gaskell and Jennings. This goes back to about the time Smith and Sharpe were splitting up and leaving Gaskell's flat.'

They read through the mails. Tony continued. 'He offers himself as a guarantor for Carla Sharpe if she could stay in the flat at a reduced rental for an extended period of one calendar month even though they were breaking their tenancy agreement. I just wonder how formal and legal the original documentation was?'

Skeeter checked the file and dialled Smith's mobile. It rang twice.

'Smith.' He sounded as though he had been working out.

'Mr Smith, DS Warlock. Sorry to trouble you so soon after our meeting. One question. The tenancy agreement you had with Gaskell. How formal was it?'

'It wasn't. It was done on a handshake and that's why he was so disappointed when we cut it short. It worked well for all of us until then that is. If it had been more formal, we'd have been buggered financially. Then we might have ended up staying together – who knows.'

'So Carla tried to stay on, extend her stay at a reduced rental?'

'Yes, I asked him if he'd let her stay as I knew I could find a place easily over on the Wirral but Carla loved the place. She couldn't afford it and I couldn't afford to help her.'

'Do you know if anyone else tried to get him to change his mind?'

'No, sorry. Not that I'm aware of. Like who?'

'Thank you, you've been most helpful.' Skeeter hung up. She looked for Gaskell's number and dialled. Tony walked over to his desk. Gaskell's phone went immediately to answerphone. 'Bugger! Make a note to call Gaskell every thirty minutes until we get through, I need to know what all that was about.'

Tony waved his hand. 'Incoming aircraft every thirty minutes ...' There was a pause. 'Nike, the note on your computer screen. Did you see the cap found near Jennings's body had the Nike thingy on it, you know, the tick?'

Skeeter stopped what she was doing and immediately logged onto the forensic report.

* * *

'I know differently. I didn't kill Jennings, or Carla for that matter. You said she wasn't dead but still missing. I've killed no one. And for your records …' he turned directly to the camera '… she enjoyed being with me, if not why would I get those calls?'

There was a knock on the door and an officer entered. Rodgers' phone and a file were in a tray which was placed in front of Lucy.

'Your phone, Mr Rodgers.' She opened the file and scanned through the text messages for the date prior to Carla's disappearance. 'Here we are. Confirms just what you've told us about receiving the message. You see, evidence is a two-way street. Before we let you go, is there anything else you should tell us under oath?'

Rodgers collected his phone and checked it. 'No doubt you'll be able to track me to all corners of the fucking globe now. No, nothing. What do they say, 'If you control some-one's SIM card, you control their life.' I wonder what you've done to mine?'

'Thank you for your co-operation. When you get outside you will in the next hour or so hear that we've found Carla's body. I offer you our condolences.'

Lucy watched his expression carefully. Fred had ensured Bill's face was turned directly to one of the ceiling cameras when the news was given.

'You knew that the moment I stepped foot in here.' His voice raised. 'Bastards! Fucking condolences my arse. You don't give a fuck, either of you and don't tell me you're just doing your job. Anything I say may be used … add that!' He turned away and was escorted from the building.

* * *

Skeeter Warlock leaned on her desk, elbows planted, her palms to either side of her face. She stared at the photograph of the black cap believed to be that belonging to Jennings. It was sitting within the grey-beige sandy soil that had powdered the peak. It was there, she could clearly make out the swoosh, the upward rising tick embroidered in black. It was subtle and almost invisible.

'Was I right?' Tony's call disturbing her concentration.

'You most certainly were.'

Just do it! If you recall that's what they told us in the advertising campaign,' Tony remarked as if auditioning for a part.

Skeeter was immediately reminded of the advertising campaign. *Just do it!* What was written on Carla's lounge wall in that copperplate type script? Her friends said it was her mantra.'

Tony stopped what he was doing. 'Give me a minute.' He brought up the forensic images of her flat and flicked through. 'Got it. *Life is for living – just live it!* Bugger me would you believe that!'

'Tell me that's not just a coincidence, Tony. Print it off and add it to the board with the two images of the caps.'

'Am I still ringing Gaskell? If you pass that brush, I'll sweep the office too whilst I'm at it.'

As Tony moved away, Kasum dropped Carla Sharpe's pathology results on her desk. 'They're on the system but there's nothing like the real thing, paper. Interesting reading. A cruel way to die – to bleed out knowing there's no one there other than the person who's just ripped your neck and throat out.' She tapped the file, turned and left. For Kasum, known for her poise and dignity, those words were in total contradiction. Reading the report, the results clearly pointed to the same type of weapon – a small piece of the tip found in part of the sternocleidomastoid muscle was being analysed. As the cut was performed on the identical side of the neck, the evidence indicated a strong likelihood it was executed by the same killer.

She quickly flicked through the results and saw the cervicovaginal smears had identified four separate male epithelial cells. It would take some time to identify the DNA and match it with friends of both victims. She read the details. Rodgers, however, was named. As she had thought, there was no evidence of the body being dragged pre- or post-death. Only superficial bruising identified on the wrists and ankles was consistent with tight binding pre mortem and shoulder damage perimortem. How they could interpret the time line was always a mystery.

'She co-operated,' Skeeter mumbled out loud as she tapped the file. The killer did nothing to the body once she was killed. 'Who else were you shagging that week, Carla Sharpe?'

Tony returned and continued in his quest to contact Gaskell. The phone was answered on the second attempt.

'Mr Gaskell? DC Price, Merseyside Police. One moment please as I transfer you to DS Warlock.'

Skeeter's phone rang and she saw Tony waving frantically. She raised her hand and then her thumb.

'Mr Gaskell, I'm investigating Carla Sharpe's disappear-

ance and we've received information that when she and
Callum Smith split, she tried to continue her occupancy of
the flat. Is that correct?'

'Yes, I mentioned it to the charming officer with the
lovely name. She couldn't afford to stay and to be honest, at
that stage, I really wasn't prepared to be charitable. An agreement after all is an agreement whether it's written or verbal.'

'That's in her report. However, you failed to mention that
you were approached by a Mr Cameron Jennings who
offered to stand as guarantor.'

'Indeed he did, but the request was only for one month
and at a reduced rate. If you read your report, you'll also see I
was fortunate enough to have a prospective tenant call at my
door not long after they left, who incidentally wanted
neither discount nor favours. It wasn't for long, four months
but then beggars can't be choosers. Strangely, Mr Taylor left
early from the contract too but he paid for the term in full.
Moved into a beautiful apartment he'd been waiting to
become vacant.'

'Did you meet with Jennings?'

'I did, yes. I met with Mr Jennings at the Costa coffee
house on Lord Street. Seemed like a nice enough chap with
good intentions. Were his actions dishonourable? You can
never tell what motivates kindness these days.'

'I believe you work on occasion with Mr Taylor?'

'It will be in the report that he gave to the police, he
mentioned you'd interviewed him. The answers will not
change if the truth is being told, that only occurs when statements constitute lies. I bought art work on a few occasions,
it's all on file. The internet is a wonderful tool for business.

He sees the space, I assess the art and if they match, we do business. There's a lot of wealthy clients and they're not all footballers in this area.'

'Do you have your diary available, Mr Gaskell?'

'Yes.'

'Will you find the fifteenth of last month, you'll see it was a Thursday.' Skeeter paused giving him a moment to find the date. 'When you locate it, can you tell me where you were from 6pm onwards?'

'Thursday, yes. I met a client at five, at a meeting on site, so it went on until about six fifteen or thereabouts. I had a dinner appointment at seven forty-five. I arrived at *The Bistro* in Formby at about seven thirty. I was back home at about eleven.'

Skeeter felt as though she were drawing teeth. 'Did you meet someone or did you dine alone?' She felt sure he would have heard the sigh that followed her enquiry.

'No.'

She waited for further information but it wasn't forthcoming. 'Mr Gaskell, we don't seem to be communicating too well so what I suggest is that I come to you and we can discuss this face to face. I'll bring a colleague too just to ensure you understand the seriousness of this enquiry. As your diary is in front of you, I'd like to make an appointment with you tomorrow at ten. Make sure you're available otherwise you'll be coming to the station for questioning. You'll be arrested. Is that clear?' Skeeter knew that she had over played her hand but it was a risk she was prepared to take.

'I was with Carla Sharpe. It was she who invited me. You are aware that when she was living in the flat, we grew quite close. Let's say she had her troubles but you know about those too. We have met on the odd occasion and she's been to my flat too. DC Warlock, I've nothing to hide and I'm happy to talk at the station or at my home. I, like you, want her home safely.'

Skeeter hung up. How could she have got him so wrong?

CHAPTER 14

Stuart Groves stared at the bronze figure of Red Rum. It had been in the Wayfarer Arcade for as long as he could remember. He had heard of the horse and its amazing success racing in the Grand National at Aintree. To think it was trained and exercised on the beaches close by. He let his eyes drift to take in the large enclosure in which he stood. The arcade was spacious and always beautifully maintained, and to come in on wet or cold days over a lunchtime was always a pleasure. The glass roof always seemed to give it a certain air of Victorian sophistication, that combined with the robust wrought iron balcony railings painted green and gold.

Collecting a coffee, he found a seat close to the statue in the central area and checked his phone. It was a text message from Carla.

Stuart, I've a free hour at two if you fancy. No worries if not. Top floor. Tulketh Street Carpark 2pm. You drive.

He consulted his watch. It was ten past twelve. Checking his diary, he realised he had a client at one and another at four. The rest of the day he had set aside for admin. He replied.

Where the hell are you? Are you okay?

The response came quickly.

I'm fine. Can we meet or not?

He returned the text.

I can but I might be five or ten minutes late. X

The frisson of excitement bubbled in his stomach as he pondered the messages. The idea of Carla in the back seat brought a smile. It was then his mood changed, dampened as he wondered where she might have been. Was she still officially missing? He sipped the coffee. Strangely, he occasionally thought about how wonderful it might be to go missing, leave behind the rat race if only for a week or so. You could contact only those you wished to contact, at a time of your choosing; no boss breathing down your neck to achieve performance targets, no, yes sir, no sir. Picking up his phone he dialled his first client.

'Mr Phelps? Ah, good, it's Stuart Groves. I was wondering if we might bring the appointment forward a little, say twelve thirty? You can? Marvellous. I'm grateful. Thank you.'

The flutter of excitement returned. He could almost see

her, smell her. Finishing his coffee, he left the arcade. Suddenly the day had taken on a whole new meaning.

* * *

The offices of KP Financial were situated in a large and impressive Victorian villa. The gardens had been partly converted into a carpark during the refurbishment. Stuart's office was on the top floor. He had described it as more of a box room to friends and family. Most meetings took place in two ground floor rooms.

Checking his watch, he had five minutes to spare. His palms were sweaty as he pulled out a can of deodorant from his desk drawer, unbuttoned the front of his shirt and liberally sprayed into each armpit. The cold stinging sensation was reassuring. His desk phone rang.

'Mr Phelps is in reception, Stuart. Shall I show him into the Clarence Suite?'

'Thanks, Marcia, I'll be right down.'

* * *

April made her way to the Incident Room. It was now the control centre for the enquiry or 'Gold' as it had become known. Skeeter and Tony were present and chatting with the man April had come to see. Their conversation stopped as she entered. She smiled and proffering his hand, the technical officer introduced himself.

'As requested, we've *pinged* both the phones. We have the log from the day before she went missing. There's the call to a William Rodgers and that checks with the report received from the interview and from his phone log. Secondly, we have identified a call to Cameron Jennings. We have that recorded but we can only assume that it's her voice. After this call it's likely the phone was cloned. Carla requested his presence at the location where his car was found. We need to ascertain if she sent it, if it was recorded and whether she was dead at that point.'

Skeeter was ready to interrupt but decided to listen a little longer.

'It's clear that Carla Sharpe's number may well have been cloned recently, possibly the same day she went missing. Our systems allow us to monitor the anomalies but as we were late in getting the permission, we can't tell when that occurred. If that's the case and the phone is cloned, the likelihood is it will be used either to send false information or inaccurate tracking info. This makes its use as evidence totally invaluable to us but vital to whoever is holding it. Cloning for the benefit of receiving calls at someone else's expense has pretty much disappeared as phones have become more sophisticated and equipment to perform the task expensive. If the person, however, has the SIM card then it's a piece of cake as you can buy a SIM reader off eBay for a few quid.'

'Spoofing?' Tony asked knowing what the answer would likely be.

'Right. As you know that means the number shown on someone's caller ID is not the actual number that's placing the call. A person can use their own phone and it mimics that of another person; they see the person's name or image come on screen and believe it to be a call or message from them when it's not. Again, it's simply a case of pulling the identifiers off the hardware. It's not illegal either in most cases.'

'So, what you're saying is that we've no way of tracking that phone?'

'Not accurately, no. What's important here is in the last hour we've managed to track some activity from Carla's phone. Brief, but it was there. We can't see what. It may even be from the other phone or the phone that was cloned. It's one of the two if that makes sense. If there was activity, we at least have a heads-up.'

'Why not get the provider to just block the number?'

'Then it would be finished. We'd have nothing. At least this way we have some intelligence. We know someone has the phone or had the phone and we'll be aware of any activity. The providers are co-operating fully and we know the phone's not been destroyed.'

'Thanks, from a technical dunce, that's really helpful, I think.' She touched his arm. 'Anything you get.' Turning to Skeeter April was about to ask a question but was brought up short.

'Didn't want to interrupt. According to the pathology report Carla Sharpe was dead before that message to Jennings was sent. Probably by six to eight hours.'

The room was momentarily silent.

'Will there be murder number three? Was that flicker of phone activity a signal, another invitation the killer is sending out?'

* * *

If Stuart Groves were keeping any sort of log, then that meeting was one of the fastest he had achieved in recent months. He believed he had conducted himself profession-ally but felt a twinge of guilt that he had not given the client his full attention. In his defence, it had to be said, he had not sold him any services he did not require. A future date for that had been pencilled in the diary. Signing out, he smiled at Marcia. 'See you in an hour or so. It's non-stop today!'

Looking at the group's diary she could see he did not have a further appointment until later. She smiled. 'You have an appointment at four ... Yes? Non-stop, right!'

He interpreted her tone and blushed slightly.

The red Audi A3 estate burbled into life and headed down the short driveway. It would be five minutes before he would arrive at the multistorey carpark on Tulketh Street. It sat at the end of a one-way system. Glancing at the back seat he smiled in anticipation.

As far as carparks went, this was generally spacious, the parking places numerous and generous. It was the upper storey, the one open to the sky he wanted. Driving up the ramp the camera recorded the registration. He would need to find a pay booth later in order to leave without incurring a fine. Midweek, there were few cars up there and those that were would have arrived early and would leave late. At the far corner, behind part of the building that towered above the upper-level brick parapet, was one large parking place. Again, owing to the distance from the exit it was seldom used. Stuart drove across the deserted roof area. The parking space was empty. He reversed in so the car's rear section was completely out of view. Remaining in the car he would watch for Carla. He was five minutes early. He watched as gulls called and circled before settling momentarily on the tarmac. It never ceased to amaze him how large and aggressive these birds were.

* * *

April briefed the impromptu meeting.

'As you're all aware, DCI Mason has successfully managed to obtain a forty-eight-hour reporting restriction on Carla Sharpe's death. Primarily it gives us time to locate her next of kin and secondly, and more importantly, for operational reasons. We now have a list of all the friends linked in the contacts of the following people: Rodgers, Smith, Jennings, Sutch and Sharpe herself. The last two were taken from their computer hardware. I'm going to question Briggs again today. If he were so infatuated with Sharpe, enough to take her name, then he might just know more than he's letting on.'

Skeeter's face broke out in a huge smile. She had forgotten about the hunch she had felt when they had spoken with him earlier.

'Anyone not interviewed from those lists, I want someone round to see them and I want it done sooner rather than later. Tony, you're coming with me to see Carlos. We'll not forewarn. Kasum, Lucy and Fred get the list sorted and start the interviews. It seems the murderer will kill either sex so keep an open mind. See if there's a reason, a link why Jennings and Sharpe were victim one and two. Sharpe was the first according to pathology so start there. Relationships, upset, broken promises ...' April let the sentence hang in the air before Skeeter broke the silence.

'Have you all seen the report added to HOLMES about the caps found at the scene? The computer had linked the two pieces of evidence but Tony and I spotted it too. Remember I mentioned Nike, the winged Goddess?' Skeeter boasted.

April turned and focused on her colleague. 'Yes, speed and victory and the like.'

'Both victims were, we believe, wearing a cap bearing the same logo, the Nike swoosh or they were both intentionally left at the scene. You may recall that Nike had an advertising campaign with the catch line, "Just do it!" Well Carla's motto for life was, and we've heard it said from her close friends on more than one occasion, *Life is for living – just live it!* It's stencilled on her lounge wall.' Skeeter held up a photograph taken during the forensic investigation of the apartment. 'For me, that's too close to be coincidence and besides I don't believe in them. Whoever killed her knew her and may have been in her apartment.'

'Have we assessed fully the touch DNA found there? That's why we have computers. Let's get onto it.' April's frown seemed to weigh heavily as she stared at the image. She stated the obvious. 'We need to find the killer before we end up with more victims.'

Nic's Nails and Beauty was busy. April entered first. Music was playing, it seemed a blend of relaxing spiritual instrumental with the occasional high pitched vocal. It was mellow and sonorous. Two beauticians were working on clients' nails. Both worked under a bright lamp. The woman on the nearer table looked up, a white, protective mask covering her mouth and nose. 'He'll be with you in a tick. Please take a seat.'

The word 'tick' made April focus on Tony.

'It's like when you buy a car, ma'am, you never saw one before you got it and then when you drive it away every other vehicle is like your new one. We'll see swooshes and ticks everywhere now. We're just more alert to them. It's normal psychology.'

The beaded curtain rattled causing them both to look in the direction of the noise. Carlos appeared and paused momentarily as he recognised Tony. He moved to the security of the reception desk. 'Police?' His enquiry was quiet as if not to broadcast the fact to the clients. 'Tell me you've found her.' His look said so much. 'Have you found her?'

'Afraid not at this stage, but our enquiries show we're close.'

'When my colleague was here previously you were asked about the last time you'd seen Carla. Can you go over that again?'

Carlos looked at Tony and then at his boss who was still busy. 'Please come this way.' He moved to a door at the far end of the room through which April could see the treatment table. Carlos flicked on the light. 'More private.' Even with the light on it was dull. 'Sorry it's subdued, it's designed to be moody. We can change the colour to suit.'

'What was your relationship with Carla, Brian?'

'She was like a mum to me.' Tears began to well in his lower lids and he took a tissue from the drawers next to the treatment table. 'When I started, I was all at sixes and sevens. It was as if I couldn't do anything right. I confused diary dates, mixed essential oils incorrectly. I was a fucking disaster. Please pardon my French. Carla obviously noticed. She sensed my discomfort and fear and she patiently guided me. She covered up my mistakes on more than one occasion. She, Nicola, was going to sack me a couple of weeks after I started but Carla, bless her, stuck up for me. That's when they started to call me Carlos. They said I was like her shadow. She taught me so much. And I owe her a lot.'

'Did you ever see her socially? Meet for a drink or a meal?'

'Only staff dos. Not … you know. She has boyfriends and I … Anyway, Callum was a lovely, handsome man; goodness me I could fancy him myself!' He giggled and brought his hand to his mouth.

'Did you go to her flat at all?'

'When they were living together in that place on Lord Street, dead posh that was too, I went there to a couple of parties.'

'Do you recall who was there?'

'Yes, I've a good memory for faces. Names though just disappear like mist in the morning. I never could remember stuff like that. Maybe a couple of names if I'm lucky.'

Carlos looked across at Tony and read his thoughts.

'I could write some down that I remember but I must warn you that my spelling is atrocious and my handwriting, you really don't want to know. Carla said I should've been a doctor as nobody could decipher it. That was one of my early problems when filling in the diary. I'm dyslexic, see. I had a shit time at school. I'm not thick, I know that, I'm more creative, arty my teachers used to say. Kids though, can be cruel.' He looked at April and then Tony as he shrugged his shoulders.

'A doctor? They're renowned for their illegible writing, I'm told.' For the first time April saw a smile. 'I will want you to come to the station with us to look over some photographs, Brian, if that's okay with your boss. You don't realise just how much you can help her if your memory is as good as you say it is. Would you be willing to do that, Brian?'

'Anything.' His expression changed immediately as he looked at his hands.

April and Tony allowed him time to think. They sensed he had been afraid to say something and they wanted to afford him some space. It was an interview technique gained only from experience when the person you were interviewing begins to feel safe enough to talk openly. They had both picked up on his body language. Brian was about to break his silence.

He turned to look directly at Tony. 'When you came in the other day you were with the officer with the glass eye? She asked me when I'd last seen Carla. You will know that I agreed with my boss, that it was the evening before she went missing, when she left here. That wasn't the truth, I'm sorry.'

'So, Brian, where did you see her last?' April asked. She rested a protective hand on his arm.

'I should have said, I'm sorry.'

'Don't worry, just tell us where you last saw her, Brian?' April asked again, her voice reassuring. Tony knew to say nothing. However, he smiled inwardly at Carlos's description of Skeeter. It was not the first time someone had made the mistake of referring to her eyes in such a way.

'A few weeks back I was telling her I was putting on

weight, too many biscuits and chocolate. She was beautiful and so slim. I knew she ran most days and she suggested I should start. I knew where she ran and she offered to run with me but I told her I was going to start walking and then build up to a jog. Can you believe she bought me some shorts and a top? That's the kind of person she was, certainly was to me at any rate.'

April glanced at Tony and she knew what he was thinking.

'Go on, Brian, she obviously liked you very much.'

'It went well and after a week I was walking and running. I needed a lot of rests but I didn't give in. On occasion we passed each other – well to be honest she passed me. She ran a circuit by Park Golf Club. Most times I'd be walking but once I was running and she came up behind me and ...' He paused, giggled and blushed slightly. 'Tapped my bottom. Cheeky minx!'

'Was that the day she went missing?'

'No, I think it was a couple of days before. On the day she disappeared I was running down Fleetwood Road just before you turn onto Park Road. Do you know the area?'

April nodded. 'Go on.'

'She had passed me about five minutes before. She paused briefly, pulled off her headphones before kissing my cheek. "Good for you!" she said and then ran on. I'll never forget that. Made me run a bit faster. As I got to the corner that's when I saw her. She was in the passenger seat of a car.'

'And it was definitely her?' April quizzed.

'Without a doubt. On my mother's life.'

Tony leaned forward. 'Did you and Carla always run in the same direction. Clockwise around the course?'

'Every time I saw her, she ran that way, yes, that's why I did the same.'

Tony glanced at April and raised an eyebrow.

'Brian, the running gear Carla bought you. What make was it?'

He flicked his finger as if making a tick. 'Nike, the one like she wore, the one with just the tick.'

CHAPTER 15

The investigation into the car seen on the webcam near the golf club entrance had so far failed to find a match to that colour, make and model, even when those with number plates closely matching some of the details had been eliminated from the enquiry. It was likely that the car for which they searched had received a false or modified number. The vehicle was probably now hidden in a garage or under cover. Michael had produced an image with the number plate as seen on the webcam and posted it on Merseyside Police social media sites in the hope of jogging someone's memory and knowledge. No details of the broken brake light were mentioned. Long shots could often prove to be successful.

* * *

Stuart Groves sat alone listening to music streamed from his phone and played loudly through his car's speakers that were attached to a holder to the right of the steering wheel. The music should have been unfamiliar to a young man, but this had been a favourite for many years. His hands beat out the rhythm onto the wheel, his eyes were closed and his head rocked to the heavy beat; the occasional tuneless lyric passed his lips. *Wishbone Ash* was not everyone's cup of tea but he had loved the album *Argus* since childhood; it was his father's favourite band. His friends had often remarked that he had been indoctrinated.

Hidden from view, the lone figure emerged from the door that led from the stairwell. He had seen the car arrive from across the road. Checking the time, he waited in the hope Groves would be settled before making an entrance. The carpark was once manned but now it was fully auto-mated and with that had come the inevitable cameras. However, they were concentrated on the cars entering and leaving rather than the parked vehicles and public's security. Over the last couple of weeks, the area had been checked for CCTV. The one pointing down Tulketh Street was not a problem; those within the lower stairwell and the one on the roof were easily avoided by simply looking down.

Sticking to the peripheral wall, he was confident he could remain out of sight of the car ensuring that Groves did not notice his approach. The high brick structure behind which the car was parked, the spot where he had been instructed to park the car, left him isolated and vulnerable. He believed his afternoon's activity would be neither honourable nor respectable so it suited the purpose perfectly. It was a good thirty seconds before Groves sensed someone standing by his driver's window. It startled him. Seeing the broad smile across the stranger's face made him relax and he stopped drumming, quickly muted the music before opening the window.

'Stuart?' The smile remained. 'Hi, good music. Carla sent me.'

'Carla?' His face changed and a look of concern spread quickly. 'She's okay?'

He nodded and rested a hand on the door frame. 'You couldn't make this up, goodness, that girl. Good job we love her, Stuart! She knows I work just across from here and she left a message to say she'd had an accident, dropped her phone down the loo. She didn't spare me the details!' He chuckled.

'That's Carla I'm afraid.' Stuart laughed, visualising her dilemma.

'So, here it is, warts and all. She got up after having a pee and she had the phone tucked in the crook of her neck. When she stood and went to flush the loo, she dropped it in the bog, not long before she was due to meet you. Women! I asked what she was doing chatting whilst ... she said, 'Don't men?' It's probably in a bag of rice as we speak drying out. Never let a woman tell you she can do two things at once, especially where a phone and a loo are concerned!' The laugh seemed genuine.

'That sounds just like her. Had she been drinking?' he laughed, hitting the steering wheel a couple of times.

'Good question, Stuart. She would never admit to it I'm sure.'

Stuart's smile quickly deserted him as he turned to look up at the stranger. 'So why not message me?'

'She said she'd tried using Twitter or something but you'd not responded. I guess she didn't want you sitting here expectantly. Don't shoot the messenger.' He smiled again moving his gloved hand from the frame and holding it up.

Groves blushed as he saw the wink and the knowing look from the stranger but did not register the latex glove. He was too caught up in the moment.

'She also asked me to give you this.'

Thrusting the raised hand through the open window he grabbed the seat belt that ran over Grove's right shoulder. He tugged it forcefully locking him into his seat. His left arm was now extended. Groves turned his head, his neck rubbing against the fabric of the belt before looking up and out of the open window. The action immediately exposed the right side of his neck. The startled and confused look quickly reappeared. The attacker had taped the weapon to his closed hand. The precaution would ensure the inevitable viscous covering of blood would not make it slip from his grasp. The bladed hand moved swiftly into the gap and penetrated the taut, exposed flesh of Stuart's neck. He struck powerfully, hitting the main target area just behind and below his left ear.

'Not laughing now, Groves, are you?'

The blade dragged forward, tearing and slicing open a red, oozing void.

* * *

Brian Briggs sat in the area set aside for visiting social workers and solicitors, it provided a better ambience and a smell of lavender, courtesy of the two plug-in air fresheners, pervaded the room. He stood and admired the long, framed photographic print of the Liverpool river front. The colours had slightly faded, and to the detriment of the image, not evenly. The area closer to the high window was almost devoid of colour.

'Your green tea okay, Brian? We're not usually asked for that but a colleague had some in his locker.'

Brian turned and approached April, holding out a hand to collect the mug.

'Lovely, thanks. Sorry! Never get tired of seeing our magnificent city.'

'We're grateful to you for coming in. I'd like you to look at the screen here with this young lady. She's our expert on facial recognition. Her name is Lynda.'

April had collected as many images she could from the Facebook friends retrieved from Carla's and Cameron's social media sites. Like pyramid selling, they quickly grew in number so if they added the friends of those friends, the list could have been endless. The decision had been taken to use only the most recent contacts.

'We've added names just in case that might jog your memory too, Brian. Just take your time. What you're doing will be a great help to Carla. Remember, you're doing this for her.'

Within twenty minutes, they had seventeen faces and names. They put the people they knew including her work colleagues, Gaskell and Smith to one side. They retained Jennings, Rodgers, Sutch and Stuart Groves, a name that had not come up before and a name that was only linked to the Facebook data of Sharpe and Gaskell.

'Do you know this man other than at the parties you attended, Brian?' She produced the printed image of Groves.

'I've seen him in the studio, not often just once or twice. Quite some time ago. A bit of a *foreigner*, cash in hand.' He looked at April. 'I don't know if I should be saying this but I regretted not telling you what I knew before so ...'

'Trust us, we're not interested in a bit of cash changing hands at this stage.'

'Carla and Nicola each had a night, an hour or so after we shut, if the work was there. Mainly it was for friends and friends of friends or when people had a special occasion and we couldn't fit them in during the regular hours. It was a back pocket type booking. It was never put in the book. He would come for some CACI treatment, that was Carla's forte. She introduced the beauty therapy, a kind of non-surgical face lift. Sometimes I'd watch and learn.'

'Did you ever watch when she was with him?' April's finger dropped onto the photograph.

'No, I was usually leaving as he arrived. He didn't come often, maybe three times at the most. There was one other, but he only came the once. That was quite a few months ago and maybe even longer. It's hard to keep track.'

He'll not be on the CCTV either, April thought.

'We don't get many men of that age in for this kind of treatment. In fact, we don't get many men in for beauty therapy at all and yet we should.'

'Could that be, Brian, because they might be getting something other than CACI?'

April watched Brian's reaction and she witnessed a metaphorical penny drop.

'You don't think ... not Carla. I refuse to even consider that suggestion. She's a good girl.'

'Right, yes, sorry for even suggesting that. And this second man wasn't in any of the images you've seen today?'

'No, I might not be able to recognise him. I saw him for a few moments and I never saw him again.'

'Was there a name?'

Brian raised his shoulders suggesting not.

'One last thing. Have you seen this man before?' She placed Simon Taylor's photograph on the desk.

Brian picked it up and studied it carefully. He shook his head. 'No. Was he at the parties?'

'We believe so.'

'He wasn't at the ones I attended. I would certainly remember that face.'

'Thank you, Brian. I'll get someone to drive you back. You've been a real help. One last thing! If you get a call that suggests it's from Carla's phone do not answer it just call me.' She passed him her card. 'Any time, do you hear?'

He read the card and slipped it into his phone case. 'Will she ring me?'

She let the question hang in the air.

April watched as he left before scribbling the words, 'friends of friends' on her notepad.

* * *

Within minutes they had tracked Stuart Groves's details and a call had been made to KP Financial.

'I'm sorry, Mr Groves is out of the office until later this afternoon. May I say who called?'

April decided Fred should go and await him at his office. They really needed to talk with him. The findings on the tests of the metal tip had come through and the update meeting in the Incident Room was due to start.

* * *

'If you inspect this, the type of blade looks innocuous enough. The twin notched concave blade is made from high quality tungsten British steel. It's immensely strong and honed to produce the perfect cutting edge. It's a blade that's designed to slice through the toughest of carpet cleanly. Inserted into the thin handle and locked by the two notches, the blade remains totally secure and easily replaced. Each time the weapon was used it would become obsolete and cheap enough to be disposable. If the knife was like this model, the blood would have crept into every nook and cranny of the handle's crisscrossed textured grip and the inside making it a forensic expert's dream.'

Tony took great delight in showing the image of the type of knife and blade used in both murders. 'Pathology has suggested this was the type of blade used considering the depth and extent of injuries seen on both victims. This is a Royal Blade, a professional carpet fitter's tool. Cheap as chips and readily available over the internet. We've requested records from the distributers for addresses within fifty miles of Southport. The blades, however, will fit any craft knife. We tend to class them as Stanley knives. We also know that our man is right-handed from the angle of the cut and dragging motion. A great deal of force would be needed to execute this kind of damage using such a blade. It's been suggested it's a hook and pull motion. Dig in hard and then drag, keeping the force against a secured neck. According to the pathologist, what you don't sever you damage. Considering the major blood vessels running within that area there's a very high chance of death resulting from the incision.'

'Wouldn't the killer be covered in blood?' Lucy asked, her face patently indicating her disgust at the method used.

Skeeter turned over one of the sheets and drew from memory the Nike swoosh logo. It was not just a line but more the shape of a handle-less blade.

'According to Forensics and Pathology it would depend on certain conditions – where you were standing, angle of the head and speed at which you could move away. So, in a confined space, yes, more than likely there'd be a good deal of blood spatter. Out in the open where you could move away quickly? Then possibly not. I don't suppose our killer was too worried about that initially. I believe it would have been considered at the early planning stage as I feel these killings were well conceived – they've a look of an execution about them to me. If he assumed that the bodies would not be found for some time, then he would have used that time to sort himself out and dispose of any evidence.'

'Surely that couldn't have been predicted in such a public carpark?' Lucy announced. 'It could have been discovered at any time.'

'It's about the location within that space and the likelihood.'

'Are there any clues as to whether we're looking for a male or female executioner?' April asked, also believing in Tony's use of the title.

'Considering the force and power needed to cause the damage sustained, there's a greater chance that the killer is male but I've known some bloody strong women in my time. I work with a couple so I'd keep an open mind. I'm sure there are people who have in the past been lulled into a sense of false security by a female and not lived to tell the story. As I say, keep an open mind.' He turned his focus on Skeeter knowing her physical attributes were more than capable of such a show of strength.

'A minute.' Skeeter stood and held up the sheet containing her doodle. 'Anyone recognise this?'

Kasum appeared. 'Groves has failed to return to his office. Not only that, he's missed an appointment which was at four and that's most unlike him according to his secretary. Fred's waiting for instruction. They've tried Groves's mobile but that's now switched off. Apparently, that's also unheard of as he's practically married to it. Today he altered an earlier appointment, brought it forward but didn't inform the secretary until the last minute. His behaviour was out of character they said and they're worried.'

'Do they know where he went?' Tony asked whilst moving back to collect his files.

'No. He'd been to lunch, met with a client earlier than planned and then dashed out again.'

April issued a series of instructions.

'Put a call out for his car registration and get it logged on the PNC. I want responses to any hits. Ensure we have co-operation with the ANPR cameras in carparks in the Southport and Liverpool areas. Emphasise that it's life critical so any reads on his registration number we need to know. Let's find him. I want the name and address of the person he saw earlier too. Has he done a runner and gone to ground or are we staring victim number three in the face?' She held up the photograph she had brought from the meeting with Brian. 'This is whom we seek.'

They each looked at the picture.

'We need to chat again with the beautiful Nicola. Something's beginning to cloud the facts. But before we close, you'll be aware that Forensics has found the titles of the films. We thought they were CDs but they were, in fact, DVDs located at the site, dangling from the scarecrow. They were: *Gladiator, Playback* and *The Revenant.* Black market copies. If you do a quick internet search or you know your films, we come up with …' she paused and waited.

'Good old "get your own back",' mumbled Tony.

'Indeed, revenge and you can add killing to the end of that. We're assured by the farmer that these were not what he used, his were damaged music CDs. We have writing on the wall. "Who had done what to whom?" is the question that should be added to the boards. Just within this small group we have a number of people who in some ways upset others. But upset enough to kill …?'

Tony waved a hand. 'One other thing at this stage. I believe Fred was making enquiries about the direction in which Carla ran her circuit. Skeeter mentioned that runners have a preferred direction. Well, according to Brian he always saw her running clockwise which matched the CCTV footage we had from the park-and-ride camera. However, the webcam clearly shows the runner we believe to be Carla running in the opposite direction. Brian confirmed on that morning she was running in the same direction as he and that was clockwise. So, we can assume she ran back towards the car as it pulled into the club driveway. She knew the person in that car. She willingly climbed in. From Brian's first-hand account, she didn't look troubled or under duress. The questions are, who was it and what made her stop her run?'

CHAPTER 16

Skeeter and April were approaching Scarisbrick on their way to the salon when the report was received.

'Stuart Groves's body has been found on the roof of the Tulketh Street carpark. The registration had been read entering at 13.51 and according to the system it's still there.'

A police request to the National Carpark Company responsible for the building to organise a computer check on the registration numbers of vehicles entering and leaving from 1pm had brought an immediate hit. They had located and reported the information within fifteen minutes of beginning the search. Such co-operation was not compulsory but was often regarded as an essential, professional and commercial duty. It might, on occasion, save lives.

April informed Skeeter of the situation.

'A PCSO was sent to check. According to his report it's gruesome. The crime scene's been closed off which will cause a few worries for those collecting cars but once CSI arrive, they'll get a route in and out to clear the place. Blue lights and horns. Let's get there.'

Skeeter's driving was as aggressive as her persona. Although the road had few clear passing places, the sound of the siren and the blue strobes were enough in most cases to allow good progress. April slipped her hand into the handle above the passenger door and forced her feet into the footwell. Scarisbrick New Road slowed their progress as they faced a number of junctions that needed careful negotiation.

Tulketh Street was clear and the light traffic was still flowing. It was only the multistorey carpark that had been closed off. Skeeter pulled up on the roadside ignoring the double yellow lines. The entry had been blocked but cars from the lower levels had been allowed to exit. It was not unusual to see a group of bystanders collecting at the scene of a crime and today was no different. Many held their mobile phones so social media would soon be awash. On this occasion they had been moved to the far side of the road to congregate on another open, ground level carpark. Occasionally, one person would be escorted into the pedestrian entry by a carpark attendant on receipt of the parking ticket. To clear them quickly, the fees had been waived and the exit barrier had been raised to ensure the vehicles were cleared from the area as swiftly as possible. The position of the body on the top floor was, if a murder can be classed as such, a convenience to those trying to keep some semblance of order below.

Skeeter heard the noise first and looked up scanning the sky in the direction of the sound. She quickly identified the distant police helicopter. It hovered in the direction of the railway line, its high-pitched drone gradually diminishing as it left the area. April and Skeeter had covered their shoes before following the designated route into the stairwell, carefully progressing from ground level and exiting on the roof. They followed the tape and cones placed to guide those attending the scene on a thin pathway until they reached a further cordon. The front of the red Audi was all that could be seen at this point. It was only when moving further round and on examining the car's windscreen did the extent of the crime become apparent. Although still transparent, there was an opaque quality to the glass giving the appearance of setting candle wax. In certain areas, the streaks and patches were darker than others. The passenger side windows were also stained in a similar way but were more difficult to detect owing to the proximity of the wall.

'Bloody hell, it's literally a shambles,' Skeeter announced. 'Someone has clearly been slaughtered.'

A PCSO was sitting on a green blanket well away from the vehicle and was being attended to by a first respond paramedic. A foil blanket had been wrapped around his shoulders; his back was against the parapet wall. April left Skeeter at the cordon and walked over. She introduced herself and crouched down.

'How's things?' She looked at the paramedic and then at the officer.

'He's fine, bit of shock considering that bloody mess he discovered. Is it hardly surprising? Fifth week into the job too. You could say a baptism of fire.' He tapped the officer's arm. 'In at the bloody deep end I'd have to say, but I guess that's the job we all face. We never know what we'll find from one day to the next. I'll leave you two and clear up. Guy in the car needs no help.'

April pulled a face to look like an accepting smile.

'Thank you, what about the blanket?' PCSO Ralph Curtis was about to stand and pull the blanket from beneath him.

'Later, I'll come back. You just relax and do as I've told you.' The paramedic stuck up his thumb and moved away.

'DI Decent. I'm SIO. Some find you've made there.'

'Don't think I've helped by throwing up over the poor sod. I've never seen as much blood in such a small space.' He paused, bringing the paper bowl that resembled a grey bowler hat from his side and to his mouth before retching. Nothing emerged. He wiped his mouth. 'Sorry! I received a call to check on a car. It was said to be in here. I started at the bottom and worked my way up. Knew the make and colour of the car I was looking for so it wasn't long before I came across it. It was just about matching the car with the correct plate number. Fortunately, I came up the ramp, over there and saw it straight away.'

'Did you see anyone leaving?'

'When I arrived to check the place, I thought it prudent to walk up the road into the carpark. It's next to that taken by the cars leaving, just in case the one I was looking for buggered off as I was entering by the pedestrian stairwell.'

'Sensible,' April encouraged although she realised the killer might well have slipped out unseen. 'Go on.'

'When I saw it, I could see the state of the windscreen. I thought it had been vandalised but then I saw the body. I've never … It was the eyes and then the blood. It seemed to be hanging from the roof lining, not like normal blood. It looked gooey, if that makes any sense, and almost deep black. The neck wound was more like the mouth and the face was the strangest thing. One half was covered in blood and the other looked like grey wax. That's when I threw up.'

'I can understand. Go on.'

'I called it in. Two members of the public helped me secure the area and within ten to fifteen minutes the helicopter was over but I guess the perpetrator was well gone. Tell me, ma'am, what kind of person does this to a fellow human being in broad daylight in a public place?'

'Between you and me, the same person who's killed two others in a fortnight but keep that to yourself.'

'Did you have your bodycam operating?'

'No, I thought I was just identifying a car. Forget the thing's there half the time.'

'Thanks. Take care. We'll be in touch. Make sure you take any support offered. These experiences have a bad habit of coming back up in here.' She pointed to his head. 'They can bite back very hard later. Have none of this stiff upper lip shit.'

'Paramedic said that. Thanks.'

April stood and walked back to Skeeter. CSI had screened the car and were photographing from all angles.

'I've requested all CCTV from here and the surrounds. The poor sod was lured here, just like the others, and it was Carla's spoofed phone I bet. I'll clear with Mason but I want the reporting restriction lifted and I want all her known friends informed individually. Somehow, Wicca, this is one we might have prevented if we'd acted differently.'

'When we arrived, I heard the helicopter and it made me think of a noise we heard when we were at Carla's crime scene. Not too dissimilar to the CSI drone only theirs was louder being closer. There was no helicopter present, police or otherwise but now for some reason I think it might have been a drone. I thought it was a motorbike when I was there, but come to think of it, the bike probably just masked it. When it had gone, so too did the noise I'd heard. Why does the idea of a winged goddess keep plaguing me? I'll nip out to Mill Farm on my way home. I have a hunch.'

'Talk to the lads at HQ, they use drones constantly as you know. Don't, whatever you do, mention the time when they lost the first one in the Mersey. I'm sure they received the usual briefing. Or the fact they were operating without permission when they made their first arrest, otherwise you'll get nowhere.' She laughed. 'I guess they received a right bollocking. Besides, the public immediately think of 1984 so they're cagey about the technology.'

* * *

He placed the coverall along with the gloves and knife within the black bin bag and tied the handle. It was small and he managed to deposit it over the concrete edge at the start of the footbridge linking Victoria Bridge Road to Back Virginia Street. The bridge crossed multiple railway tracks, and the railway banking at the start and end was heavily overgrown. There appeared to have been no one there and he dropped the bag. It vanished within the undergrowth in the area between the gardens and the track.

Moving to the centre of the bridge, the view of the helicopter announced Stuart Groves had been found. Leaning on the rough concrete his gaze followed the black-and-yellow craft until it disappeared from view. He turned his attention to the railway lines that appeared littered with boots, bottles and cans, the flotsam and jetsam of human laziness. *If they can't move that from the tracks, they'll not find what's in the bushes and brambles,* he thought. Groves was the third person. It left one more and now the challenge would begin. They were now warned, but also hopefully concerned, if not frightened. After all, that was the purpose, to do to them what they happily did to others. 'What's round comes around and we reap what we sow,' he mumbled to himself as he dropped down the steps as if nothing had happened. The last would reap the whirlwind, he was certain of that no matter what happened to him. Considering his actions of the last hour he felt quite victorious and there was a skip in his step.

CHAPTER 17

Skeeter glanced at the field that had held Carla Sharpe's corpse. There was no trace of the murder but in her mind's eye the image of the scarecrow was clearly visible. The furrows had been repaired, the blood-drenched soil turned and lost to history. The pigeons were back at work collectively searching and occasionally pecking green shoots. The deterrent had been removed. She drove on parking in the cobbled farmyard where she was quickly greeted by a woman who launched herself from the door of the farmhouse.

'We've nothing to say. The police have told us to say nothing, so please, if you're a reporter just go.'

Removing her ID from her pocket Skeeter held it out. 'I am the police, Mrs Unsworth. I met you briefly when DCI Mason called on the day of the discovery.'

She took the ID and looked directly at Skeeter. 'I remember you, the eyes. Sorry. We've had a few people telephone and a couple have turned up here asking for information. One was even seen down by the field. Worse than the bloody birds! My husband will be so angry if he sees any treading the crops!'

'The reporting restrictions will be lifted later so it might get worse. You're sure to get flowers left if gossip leaks the location ... people do both, I'm afraid. They're probably doing it with the best of intentions but it has to be said, you're a bit isolated here, so hopefully you'll not get too many. Believe me, Mrs Unsworth, it doesn't last. I need five minutes with your husband if he's about.'

'He's in the bottom barn. Come. I was taking him a brew. Fancy one, do you?'

Skeeter carried both mugs in the direction she had been instructed to take. A Jack Russell bolted from the large open doors but paused on seeing her, giving a sharp bark and then holding its ground.

'Quiet, Jack!' The instruction from within the barn made no difference. The dog barked again.

Original name, Skeeter thought as she called the farmer's name, causing the dog to run towards her.

'Jack! He's bloody soft. All piss and wind. You're the copper who was here the other day. Is one of them my brew, love? It's the Bowie eyes if that's not too rude to say. No offence intended.'

She walked forward as the dog nipped at her ankles, but he did not bite. She handed the farmer his mug. 'I was, and everyone says it, so no offence taken. DS Warlock, Serious Crime. Firstly, we've lifted press restrictions so you should expect a few unwelcome visitors. Always happens, but I didn't come here to tell you that. When I was here and we were all down by the body, I thought I heard a kind of buzzing, like a drone. I searched in the direction of the buzzing but I couldn't see anything neither did it last long. I wondered if there's anything locally that might generate a noise like that. Machinery, pumps, anything?'

Unsworth paused. 'Any relation to the old Archbishop of Liverpool?'

'No.' Skeeter sighed. This was getting to be like hard work.

'Not a common name, that.' He sipped his tea before throwing the dregs across the yard. 'Noise? Funny you asked. I thought it was my bloody ear wax. When I went to take a look that day, once the racket of the birds had calmed, I heard a similar noise. I looked to see what it was as it seemed to come from over yonder.' He pointed in the direction of a copse of trees positioned a good half-mile away, 'Could see nothing. Like you said, it didn't last long. I'd forgotten about it to tell you the truth.'

'Have you seen anyone flying a drone recently?'

He shook his head. 'No, apart from the CSI lot, but that was late in the day when you'd gone. If I had I'd have stopped them. I want to get one to check and photograph the crops. I was going to ask them, but they were far too busy. For me, I could get a clear view of areas where there's crop failure – bird's eye view, like. I read about using one in the farmers' magazines. A couple of fellow farmers I chat to at meetings have them. So, no, not seen anyone here with one. Saying that, love, I've not been looking. Haven't heard it since either.'

Skeeter reached and took his mug. 'I'll take it back. Thanks for your help. I'll have a word with the local lads to pop in over the next few days to make sure you're not pestered. Once the report goes out, they will come.'

'Aye, and they'll get a tongue thrashing if they do, love. Worked too hard on that field to get it bloody trampled ... there might be a second killing.' He winked holding up both hands. 'Kidding!'

She smiled, turned and walked towards the farmhouse. Jack barked twice but followed Unsworth back into the barn.

It was the third YouTube video she had watched as she ate cheese and onion on toast and sipped a bottle of Prospect Silver Tally ale. She had Googled "Merseyside Police Drones" and was reminded of the loss of the £13,000 drone and had a quiet chuckle. She had heard about it during training; it had occurred years before at the birth of the technology. Now it was very different, she was aware of just how efficient the drone pilots were. These tools were a vital resource when linked with the force and the emergency services. She had seen the results of their work on many occasions. From watching the videos what did impress her was the way technology had developed over such a short time and now very sophisticated drones were readily available for purchase by the general public. Many had to be registered with the CAA, but there were some that were still extremely capable that legally did not have to comply.

'Nike, the winged goddess,' she wrote down above the notes she had made, before collecting her beer and a rug that lay on the back of the sofa. She walked into the garden. The sky was a mix of colours. It was dark directly above her and awash with various shades of inky blue. Her eyes rested on the tree-topped horizon. The layer of aquamarine seemed an incongruous hue but there was clearly a line just above a fiery orangey yellow. An owl called from somewhere within the silhouetted trees as a heron flew large, its shape distinctive, its flight steady. 'Prophetic Wicca.' She watched it vanish on silent wing into the darkness.

Does this person want to be caught? she thought as she swigged another mouthful of beer. Taking out her phone she checked the signal and dialled. It rang longer than she anticipated.

'Wicca? Do you know what time it is? What do you want?' Tony's voice sounded hostile but then she heard his giggle.

'"When you're down and troubled ..."' she began to sing.

'Are you pissed?'

'No! I need to talk to a friend and a colleague. A trouble shared is a trouble halved, they tell me. I've been thinking over a few things to do with the Sharpe case.' She heard a groan.

'It's play time, Wicca. It's time to relax, watch telly or drink beer.'

'No telly, and I'm relaxed. Sitting in the garden with a beer. I need just five minutes, promise.'

'Your time starts now!'

'Ta! We have three bodies, right? Each found at different times but not killed in the order in which they were found, right? So, my thinking is, there comes a point when an act of surprise will work, when people will trust and let down their guard if they have one. However, once there's an awareness that friends or acquaintances are going missing or dying, alarm bells will ring and trust will be withdrawn. Even though we don't trust naturally, it's encouraged within today's society – it's now firmly fixed in our DNA. Kids are told to trust certain people – priests, teachers, the police, doctors. Occasionally that trust is betrayed, with dire consequences at times, but it doesn't stop the rest of us from trusting. We might be more conscious of this betrayal, but in times of what might be classed as an emergency, we trust. My question to you, my friend: do those linked in some way to this case stop trusting strangers or do they stop trusting friends knowing that the crimes are close to them?'

'If I were in that circle of friends, it would be both. I'd trust neither, strangers nor friends, until the killer is caught. Now ask me one about sport.'

She chuckled.

'Right, agreed, but if we see a smile on the face of friend or stranger, it disarms us, we drop our guard, particularly if we know them or we think we know them. When our backs are against a metaphorical wall, we need to find people on whom we can rely, and it's then that we're at our most vulnerable. People will turn to friends for support. Friends will turn to help friends and that could be their mistake. It was for Jennings and it may well have been for Groves. Tony, was Carla purely the bait to bring in the bigger fish? Is he or she picking them off one by one to instil a fear until the killer gets the person he truly wants?'

'Suspended retribution? We believe there's a strong possibility this is a vendetta. Vengeance may well be the motive considering some of the evidence but that could be a smoke screen. Open mind, isn't that what's drummed into us since basic training?'

'In my mind, the killer is like the guy painting the floor. He's started to paint, and realised he'll have to wait for it to dry to finish and leave as he's painted himself into the corner. He had all the time in the world at first to take, keep and kill. They went voluntarily as neither knew of the others' deaths and now as the news breaks the room is getting tighter. He's lost the luxury of their trust, their possible co-operation and the luxury of time.'

'Right. If you say so. I'll talk to you in the morning. Have another beer or two to take your mind off the case and put the paint brush away. Maybe Michael the magician will have developed a cunning plan.'

She chuckled. 'Thanks, Tony, for listening to the ramblings of a mad woman.'

The sky had now become a uniform black and the occasional star glinted. Finishing the dregs from the bottle she wrapped the blanket around her shoulders and stared into the darkness. She was tired but she knew the tumbling within her head would deny her the opportunity of sleep.

* * *

The booklet of photographs positioned on the table alongside three mobile phones was an anomaly. He had accurately placed and glued the images of the people taken in the pub the evening of the incident onto the separate pages. The writing below each was neat and orderly. He had slashed those early, grainy images of Sharpe, Jennings and Groves with a knife in the shape of a tick. Beneath, in a flowing hand, he had written the day and the date of death, underneath which was a small photograph of each before and during their dying moments. He had also written the words 'Life is for living – just live it!' However, on the first three, he had crossed out the words 'live it' and replaced them with the single one – 'DIE!' Below that was a description of the moments in which they died. He detailed their facial expression and noted anything they uttered. In the case of Jennings and Sharpe he noted the length of time from the incision to their final twitches. For Groves, he left the end time blank. He had needed to leave before death arrived and anyone else who needed to collect their car. 'Shock', 'fear', 'surprise', 'hurt' were but some of the descriptions. He always underlined the word 'fear' and wrote the word beneath each image.

His gloved hand turned to the next photograph, that of Bill Rodgers. Using scissors, he removed it to reveal the underlying page from which another face stared out. This face had only recently been added after careful consideration. He would be the next. He pasted Rodgers's image onto the subsequent page. It was clear, he would worry the longest.

Placing two new craft handles on the table, he inserted two blades. He positioned the dull curve of the honed edge and the fine tip facing each other.

'Eeny meeny miny moe ...' He let his finger move between the two blades until the rhyme ended. 'You are out!' On a narrow piece of tape, he wrote the name, 'Bill', before sticking it to the handle. He added what for him would be the penultimate victim before attaching that to the remaining weapon. A moment later he produced a third knife. It would be a spare in case a blade snapped. One had done, he recalled, when dispatching Sharpe.

Collecting the knives, he placed them in a shoe box.

Returning to the book he flicked through to the last page, to a photograph of Debbie Sutch. Unlike the others the words written beneath were, 'Goddess – Guardian Angels live forever!' He brought a finger to his lips before returning it to touch Sutch's mouth.

CHAPTER 18

The Merseyside Operational Command Centre based at Speke, had become a valuable modern resource for the Matrix teams. All were now housed under the one roof, a centre bristling with the necessary technology to fight today's crime in such a large and diverse city. DCI Mason flicked through the slides on the interactive board that filled most of one wall of the conference room. Today it would be open to the press. The first cameras were in the process of being organised. Occasionally he paused to read some of the notes he had prepared. His Chief Constable was not happy, not happy at all. The murders of three people occurring at the same time, he was told, was very different from what was clearly seen by the public as the strategic murder of three innocent friends. The word 'executed' had been used during his last meeting with his Chief Constable and the Commissioner. The request for greater resourcing had been discussed, balanced against the progress made to date.

Within fifteen minutes he would be interviewed by the media and he had received a clear brief as to the level of information he should make available. He was pleased that the press would not be allowed questions at this stage. For him, this building seemed somewhat alien; he would feel ill at ease until he was out of the limelight and back at his own desk in the city centre.

* * *

Carlos Briggs's world seemed to stand still when Nicola, sitting him down in the back room of the studio, informed him that Carla's body had been discovered. It was obvious from his facial expression and the pallor of his skin just how hard it had hit him. The tears seemed to squirt from his eyes as the guttural noise erupted, at the same time producing huge, uncontrollable sobs. It was so distressing it also brought her to tears. He seemed to wither and fall into her, clinging like a drowning man to the smallest piece of floating wood, desperate, frightened and for that moment, inconsolable. She quietly told him what she knew from the report she had received earlier from a DC Peet. He had introduced himself as Michael. His voice seemed controlled and reassuring but she sensed instantly he was the harbinger of bad news. He explained that he had the sorry task of informing her close friends of Carla's death. The next of kin had been notified. A statement about her murder would follow and her name released. In her heart of hearts, Nicola had expected such news. She had thought Carla might just be broken enough to have accidentally taken her own life during a bout of heavy drinking. The breakup had, she understood, been more traumatic than she had ever disclosed. The evidence was there in the way she not only lived life to the full but possibly abused the new sense of freedom. She seemed hellbent on conveying to those around her that 'Life was for living'. It suddenly seemed a false mantra.

Hearing the words 'murder investigation' dealt a huge blow. She seemed to momentarily float away from the phone conversation as if she were trying to put it all into a perspective she could comprehend fully.

'Nicola, I'm going to text you a number. It's a link to the Police Family Liaison Team. You and your staff have each other but you may also need some professional support during this traumatic time. Please, use it, it's free. Don't suffer alone. Don't hesitate to call it.'

His final statement was powerful. She had assured him she would and thanked him. He closed by offering his personal condolences.

Brian had stopped crying and lifted his head from her chest. 'I'm sorry, look, I've wet your uniform.' Taking his face in her hands she turned it so they were eye to eye.

'We need each other now, Carlos. We're going to see her and hear her in our heads. She was a massive part of your life, and mine, and she was present in this very space. We must mourn her leaving us so soon, but we must remember her in the way she would want us to. That means her laugh, her energy and her mischief. I will have her saying written on the wall in your treatment room, a room she wanted you to use. Let's say it together.'

'"Life is for living – just live it!"'

They hugged again.

'Maybe you should go home. I'll cancel your clients for the day.'

Still living at home with his mother would make it difficult for him to grieve. He refused. He realised that he wanted
to be where she once was and he felt as though she would
always be with him.

'Thanks, I'll stay. You understand me more than my mum.
Let's brush ourselves down and begin the day again. I have
clients, and what would Carla do? Live life!' They both
laughed, an inhibited and false laugh but one that was under-
standable.

He wandered into Carla's treatment room and lay on the
couch. His tears had released a torrent of emotions. He had
not cried as much since his father died but this loss seemed
even greater. She had been young and her life was cruelly
stolen from her. It was the amalgam of emotions, sadness
and anger, that helped him keep going.

Nicola's thoughts immediately turned to Smith but she
quickly dismissed any idea that he might be involved in
Carla's death. He was neither the type nor did she feel there
was any justification, if ever one could justify killing. Her
next thoughts turned to Bill Rodgers and there they lingered
for longer than she liked.

* * *

The morning light suffused the room in colour. The sun
collected the pattern from the upper-level stained-glass
windows before delicately smudging it against the white
wall. This natural phenomenon had the ability to change the
mood of the room and as a designer of living space he found
it stunning.

Craufurd Gaskell watched the traffic pass along Lord

Street, two steady streams until the traffic lights brought a halt to the flow. From his vantage point he could observe the Atkinson Gallery Clock in one direction and the Cenotaph in the other. He was spoiled. The trees lining either side were freshly leaved and vivid green. As he saw their delicate sway he thought of Carla and the officer's words in delivering his statement about three murders within his town. It looked the epitome of gentleness from this perspective, not the bosom of evil. Yes, it was now classed as part of Merseyside, but Southport had always enjoyed its own personal identity, a seaside town even though the sea was a stranger. It represented more retirement than amusement. The summer months were witness to its fair share of holiday makers but its neighbour Blackpool accommodated the majority.

Turning back to the room, he stared at the rug spread across the grey painted floorboards. He could see her. He closed his eyes in remembrance, recalling the moment he had spotted her sitting outside, opposite the apartment, looking forlorn and yet defiant. He had watched her for some time, not in a voyeuristic way; it was more fatherly, if anything. More like a guardian angel on high. Then he had seen the first spots of rain on the windows. He had gone down and brought her in just as the rain started to flush the street and pour from the protective glass canopies like miniature cascades.

On entering his apartment, she had demanded a drink before throwing cushions onto the floor and spreading herself on the rug, singing along to the song that was playing. He recalled that too as if it were yesterday – *White Flag* by Dido. He had laughed as she flicked her glass with her finger nail in time to the sound of the ringing triangle. She had then changed the lyric to 'I will surrender' before holding the glass for a refill, and looking even more upset until it was poured. He recalled that her hair was crunched in a clip. He had watched her hand move to release it. Her hair had fallen to her shoulders and she had flicked her head before unbuttoning her shirt. He opened his eyes quickly. The thought brought a cocktail of excitement, sadness and nausea. His mobile rang.

Bending to retrieve it from the table he glanced at the screen and immediately dropped the phone. Carla's image, taken on that same evening, a picture he was not proud of taking, showed as it continued to ring. A huge flush of panic ran through him. It was as if the phone had been electrified and the shock had brought this surge of guilt. It stopped ringing.

* * *

Within minutes, Carlos Briggs received a similar call. He too looked at the screen before moving it away slightly to get a clearer perspective. He emitted a scream that caused all in the salon to stare. It showed the photograph that always appeared when Carla rang – the two of them laughing.

'Are you okay, love?' a woman waiting for her nails to be done asked. 'You look as though you've seen a ghost!'

Nicola moved from behind the workstation and immediately approached him, dragging the protective mask from her face. Carlos quickly turned the ringing phone towards her. On the illuminated screen could clearly read the name, Carla, and saw the image.

'Jesus Christ!' Snatching the phone, she answered it, the

action instantly silencing the ringing. There was no one there. She grabbed her bag and removed her phone. Pausing she turned to look at Carlos. She had one missed call. It was from Carla and it had been received moments earlier. Her phone had been on mute whilst she worked.

Carlos had been warned by the police that this might happen. He took the phone back and slipped out the card he had been given. Even though he had been prepared, the sight of seeing the name appear still brought a sickening flush to his stomach. He knew now she was dead, and his upset turned to anger. He dialled the number April had given him.

It took eight minutes for the call to be connected to April's phone. She listened, assured by the calm in Carlos's voice. Noting the time and location, she thanked him, requesting he pass her number to Nicola. She asked them to contact her immediately should either receive another call. She informed the technical offer who had been working on tracking the phones. Again, there was nothing from live track to say Carla's phone had been active.

April quickly moved through to the Incident Room. There was a lot of activity but there seemed little progress. A collection of photographs removed from the three missing phones had been accessed from the cloud. April had tried to grasp the mechanics but had given up, believing it to be too abstract for her to understand fully. The contents of the phones taken from Rodgers and Sutch had also been added to the gallery. Those images containing one or more of the deceased had been collated and place and time had been configured. The decision to view all photographs for the year had also been taken. Although it meant trawling through a plethora of images, it provided a clearer picture of the group's social interaction. She sat at a computer and played through a slide show of the last known meetings to include Jennings, Sharpe and Groves.

Each image had been allocated a unique reference number. She added one of the numbers to the pad if the shot contained anyone in the background who seemed to be taking an interest in the group. It was her hope that when they were assessed, facial recognition software might identify someone known to the police. She knew it to be a long shot but at this stage when lives mattered, she was grasping at straws and prepared to use all of the resources at her disposal.

* * *

Skeeter admired the police drone that was placed on the work bench. It was the size that impressed. 'Bloody hell, Steve, I could get to Ibiza on that for my hols this summer!'

'Firstly, it's not a drone as such, it's a hexicopter. Count the prop arms. It can stay airborne even with a number of the propellors damaged or stopped owing to battery failure, making it safe to fly above crowds, built-up and sensitive areas. Litigation being what it is, you don't want this thing falling from a great height into crowds. It has multi-uses for crowd control, car chases, locating suspects and search and rescue. We use it to monitor concert crowds as it has the ability to work in both day and night situations. Not too happy in the rain, however, but we have a new one on test that will be! This one can lock onto, and follow, a subject using a number of clever, technical components. These three domes,' he pointed to the concave cups positioned on the three stalks that sat on the top of the machine, 'allow it to link to a number of satellites and is accurate to a centimetre. It knows where it is in the world at all times and so do I when it's flying out of sight. Back here at our base, all of that information is logged in real time and analysed to enable me to guide it.'

Skeeter raised her eyebrows as she looked carefully around the machine.

'This camera here,' he pointed to what appeared to be a small black box, 'is a Z30 meaning it has a thirty times optical zoom. I'll demonstrate later. This is an XTR thermal imaging camera, it's radio metric ...' He stopped as the confused look appeared on her face. 'We can pick people and animals out in the dark. Come on, we'll fly it. You need to see it for real.' He tossed her a high visibility jacket, a hard hat and some safety goggles. 'Elf and safety. It's the law!'

The copter stood on a spot marked 'H', a dedicated pad used for checking and calibrating. Skeeter watched as Steve conducted a pre-flight check before returning to the control panel. Slipping the straps over his head the panel sat on his chest.

'You see the red flashing lights?'

'Yep.'

'It's going through a sequence checking all its systems before flight. When they turn green, Amy's ready.'

'Amy?'

'I've called it after Amy Johnson, the British aviatrix. Nice eh?'

'She died on her last flight from Blackpool. Probably flew over where we are now if my history serves me correctly. Brave woman.'

'I didn't know that. Knowing that now, maybe I should change its name.'

The copter climbed effortlessly into the air and the undercarriage lifted two stork-like legs to the horizontal making Skeeter chuckle before it hovered above them. The sound was not as intense as she had expected.

'We have to be conscious of Liverpool airport. This building is on the old airfield site but otherwise we can go to four hundred feet. It's got its own transponder and those in air traffic can see and identify it as ours and therefore know it's legitimate.' He removed his hands before waggling them and grinned almost childlike as the drone hovered freely. 'Well, not always! It will stay there until the batteries nearly run out and then it'll return to the point of take-off.'

'Can you take it just out of sight so I can listen for it, Steve?'

The copter flew rapidly behind the building, climbing steadily.

'Find it!' Steve announced as Skeeter checked the sky. She could hear the light droning but it was generally lost against the surrounding buildings. The noise, however, was not too dissimilar to that she had heard at the farm.

'Nope. Can't see it.' She swivelled her head trying to locate it through the sound.

Within minutes, it hovered above them, and the legs lowered in tandem with the descending craft before it touched down on the 'H'.

'That's it really. Apart from training, getting a commercial licence, experience and good looks!' He winked as he removed the controller from around his neck. 'And you also owe me a beer!'

Skeeter chatted for longer than she had planned; she liked Steve. Once back inside they looked at the amateur footage showing the discovery of Jennings's body, taken from the drone.

'That was probably an early drone looking at those images. The camera quality is very poor. We face a lot of issues with people flying them either too high or too near restricted areas. Like all things, you'll always get those who flout the rules.'

They looked through the file and found the pilot's name and his address.

'Interviewed on the day at the site. Took his micro SD card. Was that ever returned?'

Skeeter scrolled down the report. The receipt had been issued but it appeared the card was still held at Forensics. 'They were trying to enhance the images, I believe.'

Steve shook his head. 'They can do the impossible, but miracles? Sorry, that's a compromised film, it'll just pixilate.'

Skeeter made a note and tucked it into her pocket. 'I've taken too much of your time. Thanks.'

'Anytime. You know where I am. Don't forget to book me when you decide to fly to Ibiza and don't forget the beer!'

Skeeter stuck up her thumb. Once at the car she entered the postcode of the address she had jotted down from the report. She would collect the micro SD card and then a visit would be in order.

CHAPTER 19

Simon Taylor crossed Canada Boulevard at the Pier Head and found the bench facing the statue of Edward VII. It was not the best of views as the Mersey Ferries building blocked the panorama of the river frontage. However, this was the location Craufurd had requested and it was within easy walking distance from his apartment. He sipped a coffee he had collected on route. The area in front of the Liver building was always a busy promenade, what with the relatively new statue of the Beatles and the exposed canal it attracted both workers and tourists alike. Facing south also had its advantages. Today was no exception and the warmth and the bounce of the light from the grey granite sets made it a pleasant place to sit.

To hear someone shout they were on George Parade and it was obviously named after George Harrison brought a smile. He hoped they would go on to find John Street, Paul Street and Ringo Starr Drive but he doubted they would bother. From the corner of his eye, he saw Craufurd approaching.

'Thanks for meeting me.' He took a deep breath. 'What a bloody last few days. I suppose you've heard about Carla?'

'On the news. Dangerous area you live in at the moment, my friend. I believe you've met them all? Jennings was it? Then there's this chap, the latest. Discovered on the top of the carpark. Glad I moved, Craufurd. Much safer. Cop shop almost next door too.' He smiled and sipped his coffee. 'What can I do for you that we couldn't manage over the internet?'

'I have a painting in the car I'm interested in selling. I could put it through auction but you know how long-winded that can be. It's too big to carry here. It's in the carpark on Princes Parade.'

They both stood, Simon dropping his coffee cup into the first litter bin.

* * *

The drive from Speke to Waterloo via Copy Lane Police Station was quicker than Skeeter had expected. She had elected to take the M57 and avoid the city centre traffic. The houses along Tudor Road were not what she was expecting. Not all of the houses were designed the same, some had an Art Deco feel, many were painted in cream or magnolia. Their curved frontage gave them a genteel appearance. However, it soon became clear the house for which Skeeter searched was not in the same league. It stood out like a blackening tooth in a white smile. She parked at the front and checked the address. A large tree looked to have punctured the tarmac and shaded the frontage.

The gate hung on one hinge; the painted wrought iron was scaled and flaking. The garden was overgrown but still retained a vestige of design. Skeeter noticed the curtain of the house next door move as she approached the front door. The curved window to the left was blinded by yellowing net curtains that rested on the inner window sill. A number of dead flies were trapped in the folds. She knocked on the door before glancing round. Moving away, she looked up at the bedroom windows and then the guttering of the over-hanging roof. Rosebay willowherb had taken hold along its length. Skeeter moved under the semi-circular door cover and knocked again.

'He's out! Out since early doors. Always out.'

Skeeter turned to address the neighbour. She had progressed from lifting the curtain to monitor the move-ments of a stranger to direct confrontation. As a police offi-cer, Skeeter was impressed.

'What time did he leave, and more importantly, what time does he get back?'

The difference between the two properties was marked. The front was unpainted but pebble dashed, the hanging baskets were ordered and recently planted and the garden immaculate. You could tell there was no car in the household as the drive comprised different ornaments and pots.

'Are you Social Services?'

Skeeter shook her head. 'No, just need some help.'

'Help? Come to the wrong address there then love. Your eye looks sore. Can't help himself let alone others. Look at the state of the garden. Wasn't always like this. When his mother was alive it was beautiful, best on the road. She was so precise and when she passed away her son just let it go to this. No concern for anyone else.'

Skeeter knew from the report that he had not worked for

some time. He had referred to his depression when first interviewed, detailing the trauma stemming from his mother's death. He had stopped working at Jaguar, Speke around the same time. She was also aware there was now no car registered to this address.

'My name's Skeeter. I used to work with him. And you?'

'Joan, love. Pleased to meet you. Shall I tell him you called?'

'No, I'll pop back. Could you give me a ring when he returns? I'd love to surprise Trevor if I can, sooner rather than later.' She jotted down her number and passed it over the fence.

'I'll need my specs. I'll do that, love.'

'Surprise remember, Joan, love.' She just had to add the word 'love'.

'You'd think working at Jaguar he'd have a car. We get discount.'

'Bicycle, one of those electric ones. Goes everywhere on it laden to the gunwales some days with bits and bobs.'

Simon Taylor stood back from the estate car as Craufurd opened the tailgate. The rear seats had been folded flat. A large object rested beneath a tartan rug. Flicking back the corner, Craufurd exposed the high gloss abstract art work. He immediately raised his eyes to look directly at Taylor.

'Can we prop it against the back?'

The painting was removed and placed so the light from the gaps running along the edge of the building flooded onto it. Once positioned, Craufurd moved to stand at Taylor's side.

'I've been redesigning some offices and this was in their boardroom. The colours are just not appropriate for what they had specified and so when the new work was installed, I bought it. It was just too good for the skip!'

'So why the intrigue – "I'll bring it and meet you."' His voice mimicked Craufurd's. 'We usually deal on the net. If the price is right you know I'd have bought it.'

'I needed a word, face to face.'

Taylor turned away from the picture.

'Have the police paid you any visits regarding Carla Sharpe and the apartment?'

A car passed and they both moved to the side.

'Yes, they were curious about my friendship with Carla and Smith but they were also asking about Jennings. I'd met them, of course, at the parties. I told them, too, how I first met her. Couldn't believe it when I read it was murder. Such a bloody waste.' Pausing, he moved and focused on the art work, momentarily allowing his finger to rub the high gloss sheen. It was cold to the touch. 'Three now I believe, and all three came to your apartment – well, technically, it was their apartment if we're being pedantic. You could have asked that on the phone.'

Craufurd moved closer. 'That's true, Simon, very true but then …'

* * *

Skeeter had just turned approaching Copy Lane, when her phone rang.

171

'Is that you Skeeter? It's me.'

'Joan, love?' Skeeter answered.

'Yes! Joan, love. He's back. I've not said anything. He's put his bicycle down the side of the house and into the garage at the back.'

Skeeter wasted no time. From her present position it took her only fifteen minutes to return.

The same curtain twitched, identical to the circumstances of her first visit, but then a small hand appeared and Joan raised a thumb as if signalling all was well. Skeeter chuckled to herself as she knocked on the door. It was then she sensed she was being watched by someone close. Leaning to look back at the neighbour's window she saw the curtain was no longer strained to the side. It was on turning back she saw him standing some way from the front window, the gap in the net curtains slightly parted. Skeeter stared back before producing her ID and slapping it against the window. The figure moved forward and looked. Nodding his head, he immediately vanished from view. Seconds later, the door opened. A smell of bacon escaped and took refuge in her nostrils making her mouth water.

'Trevor Thomas? That's a welcome aroma. Not had a bacon butty for quite some time.'

The non-threatening interaction brought a smile. 'Is it about my video? You still have my micro SD and they're not cheap.'

From her pocket she took a plastic forensic bag. His name and the date received were clearly marked. 'Long overdue, sorry. May I have a minute of your time?'

Trevor moved to one side directing her to the door to the left of the hallway. It was neither conventional nor was it what she expected. The walls were organised with aerial images, many seemingly out of focus but still fascinating. She instantly recognised the Gormley figures situated along the coast, many submerged at various depths. Then there was an aerial picture of the lighthouse at Fort Perch Rock, New Brighton. From the ceiling hung models of aircraft, each meticulously painted. They encapsulated a history of aviation and she immediately thought of Tony and his paper dart.

Trevor pulled a chair from behind a desk. She realised it was where he had been when she knocked. He invited her to sit. He looked directly at her. It was a rare occurrence when someone did not find eye to eye contact uncomfortable.

'How may I assist you on this occasion?' There was no hint of an accent in his voice, certainly there was no Scouse lurking within the vowels. 'Strange affair, that. I haven't returned to that area with my drone.' He pointed to the machine on the desk.

'To be honest, Mr Thomas, I'm not surprised. No, it's not really to do with that, just taking the opportunity to return your property. I must tell you it has been formatted as I'm sure you wouldn't want to keep the images you witnessed. I just thought I'd ask about that.' She pointed to his drone. 'Since this case I have to admit to being fascinated by them.'

'This is a cheap one. I'd love one of the new models but since mother passed and with losing my job, it would definitely be a luxury I can't afford.'

'My condolences, I'm sorry for your loss.'

'They were kind at work and kept me on but I felt I was a drain and a burden so I quit before I was pushed. Like life really. I was just putting some coloured decorative film on the drone, makes it more personal. You can get all sorts of patterns now and it's cheaper than a new one.'

Skeeter stood and studied the patterned design on part of the machine. A craft knife sat nearby and she felt the hairs on her arms rise.

'You'll certainly see that coming!'

'They're so hard to see when they're against foliage so I thought I'd try this.' He picked it up. 'Weighs nothing but will travel at twenty-five miles per hour. Hover at the same spot unaided until the battery fades and then it will return home – to the spot it started from. If only the camera was better.'

She recalled Steve saying the same thing.

'You could set that to hover and go off for a coffee, and when you returned it would still be sitting there at the height you set?'

'More or less. Seventeen satellites control it. The newer ones are even better.'

'Where do you fly, Mr Thomas?'

'Usually where there are no people. That spot near Southport was wonderful. The countryside is lovely too.'

'Have you ever flown near Midge Mill Lane?'

There was an immediate sense of tension as Thomas looked away. 'No, no. Where's that?'

Skeeter explained where it was but he informed her he had not flown there. He quickly changed the subject.

'I see you have three dead now. It was in the news, on constantly, but now? It's as if they never existed. Like mum. At first, she was always in my head. This place was beautiful when she was alive, she lived for the garden. Nature soon takes it back.' He moved to the window and lifted the net curtain. The carapace of what appeared to be a large spider dropped onto the sill to add to the collection. 'All that hard work. This was beautiful all year round. You can ask anyone on here. But now she's gone, it's gone with her. It's as if she was never here sometimes and that's what I find hard. I still have all her things and I've not touched her room. Just haven't got the will or the inclination. Have you ever lost someone close?'

Skeeter knew not to get involved; she was neither a social worker nor did she really care enough to enter into conversation involving personal matters. The neighbour had made her aware of his mental instability and from this brief exchange with him it was clear he was treading a personal tightrope of frustration and guilt. She was not a psychologist but she knew confusion and resentment were often the traits seen in both victims and perpetrators. She had discovered what she had come for but her curiosity demanded more time.

'You could garden, surely. The fresh air would do you good, and you'd see the benefits of your labour.'

He turned dropping the curtain, disturbing the dead flies and insects yet again, in some cases enshrouding them in yellowing netting. 'It's dead time gardening, I told her that.'

'And what did she say?' Skeeter laughed as if to make light of the situation. The mood was changing.

His facial expression did not alter.

'She said I was just like my father.'

'Was that wrong?'

'No, he never did much other than watch TV and go to football. She used to say I needed to find the love of a good woman too but …'

'Do you have a lady friend, Mr Taylor?'

'Thank you for the micro SD card.' It was his turn to change the subject.

'One last thing. Do you own a car?'

'Used to when mother was alive. Took her on trips, shopping, and I used it for work. It's unnecessary now.'

As she left and walked down the short drive, she felt again as though she were being watched. Approaching her car, she turned. Now the curtains in both houses had taken on a pulse of their own and twitched almost in harmony.

* * *

Craufurd's inquisitorial expression made him look angry. Red blotches had appeared on parts of his neck. 'What did you say about Carla and me?'

Taylor laughed out loud. 'That's what this is about. That's why you're so hot under the collar. I told them what I saw, I told them about seeing you both in the restaurant in Formby. Was that wrong of me?'

'It's what else you've told them that causes me distress.'

'I mentioned nothing. That, sir, will remain between the two of us. Let's say we had a gentleman's agreement. I wouldn't tell, if I didn't pay the rest of the rent. It was as simple as that. Am I in danger of losing my life in a carpark in Liverpool, Craufurd? Did you kill them?'

The transparent beads of sweat mimicked the gloss on the picture, reflecting both natural and artificial light as Gaskell leaned against the car. 'No,' he turned to Taylor. 'I didn't.'

'I know that's the truth. Now, shall we do business? You know your sordid secret's safe with me. How much?'

'Bloody hell. What do they say? Takes all kinds to make a world. He's definitely one mixed up young man. My mother would say spoiled rotten but ...' Skeeter grumbled as she leaned on the door frame to April's office.

April looked up from the files she had been studying whilst cross-referencing the facts she had on screen. 'And who's that?' She placed both elbows on the table whilst resting her chin on her hands.

'Trevor Thomas, our drone pilot from the Jennings's case. Something had been nagging at me since hearing that noise whilst standing at the Sharpe crime scene. I know you heard it but then Mason didn't, and I began to doubt my own hearing. What with this damage!' She pointed to the cauliflower ear. 'To me Mason was too much in a bloody flap to hear anything. The farmer had heard it before we arrived. He thought it was a drone too. "A winged goddess flying over the battlefield ... the Nike caps."' Skeeter spread her arms and moved further into the room as if gliding and brought a depth to her voice as she replied.

'Very dramatic but no Oscar on this occasion. Why risk being caught? It's pushing your luck if you were seen at the murder site of two people. Coincidence would fly straight out of the window and no pun was intended.'

'There are plenty of cases where the killer keeps returning to the scene of their crimes, a bit like the butcher bird – hangs its prey on thorns within hedgerows to return later to gorge itself. As you say, using that analogy, then maybe he's going back as a winged god over his battlefield.'

Skeeter moved further into the office, folded her arms and stared at April. One part of her thought the likelihood somewhat remote, whereas another seemed strongly convinced he had a role to play.

April tapped the keys on her computer and instantaneously the printer to the side of her desk spewed out a sheet of paper. 'You might want to look at that seeing you've mentioned your goddess, Nike.'

Skeeter leaned over and collected the page. In bold, black letters the following words were printed:

Destroy to Create

She read it a couple of times before turning it round. '*Qu'est-ce que c'est?*'

'It's something Michael trawled up. A number of years ago the Nike company ran a campaign. It concerned special jackets they made, or had made, in the past, he thinks, and that was the slogan. If you check the web, you'll see some of the videos. Destruction for the sake of it really but if you feel there's a relevance with the swoosh and the logo then that should have a place within your thought processes.'

April stood and stretched whilst tagging her hands into the small of her back. 'So, Thomas?'

'From what I see, he has lived alone since the death of his mother. Checking the details, he no longer works but we knew that so I've requested information from his last employer. The neighbour mentioned mental health issues brought on by his mother's sudden death. Heart attack, allegedly. Depression, the neighbour thought, and considering the radar system she has at her property, she knows a good deal. As we are aware, he was into drones in a big way. But from the room I was in it's obvious he's fascinated by all things aeronautical. Plastic planes were suspended from the ceiling of what might well have once been the lounge. I'm not talking of one or two either. All beautifully made, dusty but accurate.'

'Is he our killer?' April asked as she returned to her seat.

'Good looking chap who's just gone off the tracks. To think of it, history is littered with people like him, and yet only a minute percentage are proven criminals let alone killers. They're just sad.' Skeeter chuckled to herself. 'I really did freak out a little when I saw the craft knife on his desk. A box of new blades too. It was only when I saw what he was doing did I relax; it was the right equipment for the job. They were the straight blades too! Had they been the curved type I'd have been out of there like a shot.'

'I can see it's caused you some degree of upset.'

Skeeter was about to leave. 'Not upset, no. Confusion, great confusion. You've felt it yourself I'm sure when some things seem like one thing but then they're not what you originally thought. Can I keep this?' She waved the recently printed sheet.

'No problem. There's one on the boards in the Incident Room alongside the cap images and the advertising quotation. Before you go, there's something else. We've identified twenty or so photographs taken from the cloud, linked to the three missing phones as well as those from Debbie Sutch and Bill Rodgers. You can see that each photograph depicts the collective of friends – those within the group apart from the one taking the photograph.' She looked up as Skeeter now perched on the edge of her desk. 'Checking those people caught in the background we see the same face three times. On each occasion he's staring directly at the group.'

'Photo bombing?'

'Too far away. Facial recognition has confirmed it's one and the same person but as yet we don't have an identity. They're going to enhance it magically so we can get it out to the public.'

'Carlos and Nicola received those spurious contacts from Carla's phone. Did Rodgers?'

'If he did, he hasn't reported it. Maybe he deleted her from his contacts straight after he was interviewed, and therefore it wouldn't show under an image or her name, it would only show as a call.'

'It would show a number,' Skeeter fired back.

'Did he know her number? We rely now on just seeing the name. I ring you. What's my mobile number?'

'I'd have to look.'

'I rest my case. Still wouldn't trust him as far as. What about Smith?'

'We know he had her number.'

April flicked through a file and telephoned Smith.

'Smith!' His answer was direct.

'Mr Smith, DI Decent. A number of your old friends are receiving spurious calls from a cloned phone. They're shown to be coming from Carla Sharpe's mobile. Have you experienced this?'

'Twice. Put it down to nuisance as one of your colleagues advised. Deleted all contacts relating to her. Social media too.'

'And who was that colleague?'

'I think his name was Michael, called me the other evening. Surprised at the late call to be honest. Advised I delete the contacts and explained. Is that okay?'

'Yes, just checking. We've had a few more calls made since.'

'Why not just close down her phone and then the cloned one will cease to be of value?'

'It's not as simple as that, Mr Smith. Thanks for your co-operation.'

Skeeter held up her hand and signalled she wanted to speak to him.

'Just a minute my sergeant needs a quick word.' She handed the phone to her.

'DS Warlock. Thanks. You held a number of parties when you were at the apartment on Lord Street. Do you have any photographs of these or know of those who attended who might have? We all have friends who don't live in the moment. They spend their time behind a screen capturing it for posterity but then never look at it beyond a couple of times?'

'Yes, I have some. I can send them on if you give me an email address. I'll add the names and numbers of those people you rightly mention. Give me an hour. My photographs are on a hard drive at home and not entirely filed in order.'

Skeeter gave him her work's contact email, thanked him and turned to April. 'Your spectre at the feast might just have attended one or two parties.'

April nodded and smiled. 'How very true. Well done you!'

The forensic results had confirmed the soil sample taken from the shoe found on Jennings was a match for the soil type where Sharpe was found. It was clear that the killer intended to and had successfully linked the two deaths. The reason, however, would remain unknown. There was always the possibility that the killer wanted it to look as though Jennings killed Sharpe but then it was unlikely that he cut his own throat, particularly in light of the pathology results. The details were logged in the hope some further evidence might show a more positive link.

'So, what do we do about Trevor? How strong is your instinct on that? Is he a potential wrong one – a killer?' April's attention turned back to the misgivings Skeeter had harboured in the first instance.

'When I asked about Midge Mill Lane he clammed up, did the dance, the shifting of feet you often see when a question surprises someone, takes the wind from their sails. There's something there, but enough to justify a search?' Skeeter was conscious of resources and could not justify a full warranted search when all they were dealing with was a man with an unstable mental condition. She shook her head. 'At present, no.'

'Suggestion. Take the officer you've been chatting to about drones with you. Make the excuse you thought Trevor might be interested in the police technology in that developing field of work. He could take one with him and get him chatting. It's non-confrontational and he might just open up. It's a slowly, slowly approach and would take an hour, but might answer the nag you clearly feel.'

Skeeter rubbed her chin considering the idea, and her head began to nod in agreement. 'I'll organise it.' Waving the sheet, she left. 'Thanks. That's why you're the boss.'

* * *

The decal had been created, a large transfer in blue copperplate script. It was loosely rolled and Nicola's partner, Jim, carried it under his arm as he called at the salon. It was quickly unrolled before spreading it along the floor.

'The things a man does for his woman,' he muttered as he leaned over and kissed her cheek. 'Was that what you wanted?'

Carlos and Nicola stood motionless and looked at the offering, before silent tears appeared to both their eyes.

'Bloody Hell! You told me it was a positive mantra: "Life is for living – just live it!" Here you both are blubbering. Am I putting it up or not?' He looked at Carlos and then at Nicola.

She moved back to him and gave him a hug. 'When it's in

place it will be. We need to live with it for a while don't we Carlos?'

Carlos entered the treatment room and the two men began to move the couch and the side tables. Nicola went to make a drink.

Once the horizontal chalk line had been levelled across the wall, Jim carefully unrolled the decal. He smoothed the surface with a squeegee to remove the air bubbles trapped beneath. Working steadily, he removed the backing so the adhesive made contact with the wall. Carlos sat on the floor and watched. It was then he noticed the small, red notebook attached with tape to the underside of the chest of drawers that normally sat next to the treatment couch. He had used the drawers on many occasions, he had even cleaned the chest, but he had never noticed the notebook. Moving across, he took hold of it, pulled it off and flicked through a couple of pages.

'Carlos, I need a hand to roll this along. What have you found?'

Thinking quickly, he stuffed it into his back pocket as he stood to take hold of the remaining roll. 'I've been looking for that for ages, a notebook. Must have been trapped between the drawers. I'd looked there too. Must have been a man look!' he giggled.

Fifteen minutes later they were sitting with a coffee and admiring the mural.

'You can't get more positive than that,' announced Jim as he drank the last dregs from his mug. 'Come on. I need a beer. It's been a long day. Coming?' He turned to Carlos.

'No, no thanks, I'll just close up here. You go. I'll spend

ten minutes or so here just to finish rearranging my new and now positive treatment room.' His smile was genuine.

'Don't you stay late.' Nicola moved across and kissed him. 'Don't forget the alarm too.'

Once they had left, he slipped his hand to his back pocket and retrieved the notebook. Opening it, he found it contained a series of doodles. Clearly, they were Carla's, sets of initials and a series of numbers and dates. One set seemed to be crossed through. He thought he knew what the book was for and a cold uncertainty crept through him.

CHAPTER 21

There had been no contact from the general public to identify the image posted of the face identified on three of the group photographs. Smith had forwarded images and the names of his contacts. They were evidence of the number of people who attended the parties held at the apartment on Lord Street. The team was now not interested in the individuals they had identified, more those that were unfamiliar. In particular, they hoped the face seen on the group images could be spotted here. The photographs had been dated, and that helped in separating the varying parties and possibly the different guests. Lynda, from Facial Recognition, was given the task of searching the faces. She relished the thought of finding the proverbial needle in the haystack – a face in a crowd. It took her less than an hour before the results were coming in and new faces were identified. They had contacted Callum Smith and any unknown faces were sent to him for possible identification. Those that he could not identify were sent to the other guests Smith had named. It was going to be a process of elimination. It was soon clear that the identification of a few would prove difficult.

Debbie Sutch was contacted, and so too Bill Rodgers. The final roll of the dice, should they need, would be to seek the co-operation of Gaskell, Briggs and Taylor, all of whom were known to have attended or had been seen at one party or another.

Having the names, and then locating addresses, was solid police craft, now helped and made quicker, more accurate and easier by computers. What would have taken days and many man hours in the past, could now be done quickly and efficiently. They ended up with four unknowns. Each face was also run through facial recognition software to identify any link with past crimes. The human face was fast becoming as accurate a forensic tool as the fingerprint.

* * *

Carlos flicked through the thin red book. The initials were clear, CJ, FL, CG, BR and PW. The only names that came to him from the initials were those of Cameron Jennings and possibly Bill Rodgers. He checked the dates next to the names and he recalled seeing both men on dates near their names. One of the other sets of initials must have been the person whose face he saw briefly but failed to recognise when at the police station. FL could well have been the one, as he appeared to have only the one date to his page. A line had been struck through the initials and an indecipherable comment and a zero marked beneath the date. The others seemed to have either 7, 4, 6 or 10 against their visits. This was undeniably Carla's record of the clients who had called for treatment after hours – her little red book. The dilemma for Carlos Briggs now was, what to do with it.

* * *

Skeeter and Steve walked down the drive. She had called the neighbour to check Thomas was in. She received the thumbs up from a hand protruding from behind the curtain before it quickly vanished. Steve carried a hard, grey case. She knocked on the door and looked through the windows like last time. When Trevor saw her, he recognised her immediately. Even so, he opened the door on the security chain.

'Trevor, this is Steve. He works with the police and he flies the police drone. I thought you might like to see it and have a chat as we were in the area.'

There was an immediate change in demeanour as the door was quickly closed and then opened. They were welcomed inside. The first thirty minutes fascinated both Trevor and Skeeter as Steve went through the drone's capabilities. It was the latest version and one that the police were trialling. Steve had decided to come around to talking about aerial filming once a rapport had been established. He looked at Trevor's drone, suggesting ways to improve the image quality using the settings mode on the handset. It was during this conversation that Trevor let his wish slip about having a better zoom facility on his camera. He talked about the incident near the farm he had accidentally witnessed before showing Steve some of the still images.

'Was that near Downholland, Trevor?'

'I was there early just flying around. I like to cycle out to different places. I go early to catch the good light. It's quiet.'

He turned to Skeeter. 'That's how I got mixed up with finding that body. Here you see the tractor in the distance. For some reason some emergency services arrived. You can see the flashing blue lights. I was curious but kept the drone away as it's unlawful to fly near such a situation. I thought someone had had an accident. I brought the drone back and waited. I could see from where I was and within an hour or so, a number of others arrived. I sent the drone out again to photograph and video but when I tried to enlarge the images, they pixilated. If it had been a 4K camera it would have been better and if I'd had that, wow!'

'Do you know what you were witnessing?'

'No, unfortunately my batteries were running low so I had to pack up. My drone should fly for thirty minutes but the batteries are getting long in the tooth and they don't hold the same charge they once did.'

Steve looked at Skeeter. She could see from his expression this man was not the killer. The poor sod had found himself at a murder scene twice by pure coincidence.

I never believed in that, not until today. Let's hope these things don't come in threes, she thought as she watched Steve pack away the equipment.

'Hope you enjoyed that, Trevor. Maybe I could organise for you to see it fly one of these days. It's as easy to operate as that one of yours. Don't forget to try the camera settings I've suggested, you just never know.'

Steve closed the lid of the case and they both moved to the door.

'Thank you. As my mother always used to say a promise is really a debt. That was so kind of you to remember me. It was very informative and enjoyable. Anytime you're passing you'd be most welcome. I don't get many visitors so your surprise call has made my week, thank you.' He waved and turned to go back inside. As he closed the door, a smile crossed his lips.

Skeeter rang April. 'Good plan of yours to have a social chat with Trevor rather than come in with the cavalry all guns blazing. Neither of us thinks he's our man. Just in the wrong place and the wrong time – twice!'

Carlos waved as he left the salon for lunch. It was just after one thirty, later than usual. Nicola watched him leave. He seemed such a sad man. Gone was the bounce in his step he had always shown when Carla was around. However, she knew it would return – time would heal the wound.

The Atkinson Gallery was busy, and a party of school children loitered around the shop, their sharp, excited voices echoing in the cavernous void. An old red car was parked further into the building and he read posters linking it to some speed record held way back in time. He had never been interested in cars, even as a child, and this one was no exception. As a matter of curiosity, he did walk around it the once. He could smell the oil, obviously leaking from the old motor. On looking beneath, he saw the metal catch tray and the small puddle of shiny black. Turning to his right he entered the café. It would be his usual order: a one-shot latte and a toasted teacake with extra butter.

The waitress recognised him immediately and she gave a warm, welcoming wave. 'Where you sitting today, Brian? I'll bring them over. I know you like your coffee piping hot.

You're looking a bit better.' Her smile was immediate but it was tinged with sadness.

Carlos checked the empty seats before choosing a table by the far wall. He pointed.

'That's number eight. You should know them by now. Won't be a tick.'

As he sat, two more people entered. The room, once a large part of the building's grand entrance, had recently been divided into more functional spaces. The height of the ceilings had been maintained and the large windows reflected the building's grandeur. The heating pipes and the electrical conduit had been left exposed, giving the space a more industrial yet modern feel. There was always a buzz about the place, what with the theatre, the library, the art gallery and museum situated on the same site. It was all things to the citizens and visitors to the town, particularly on wet and windy days.

He watched as the customers both paused on entry, as if searching for someone. Initially Carlos thought they were together, but he was wrong. The man, in his late twenties, went to the counter and an elderly woman had, after a moment of searching, spotted her companion. She waved before moving towards their table. The man, now at the counter, turned and looked directly at Carlos before collecting his drink. He waited for his change and then moved to sit at the next table, number seven. He nodded as he sat. He said nothing but stirred his coffee. Within a minute the waitress brought Carlos his order, the butter melting and forming golden pools on the plate.

'Brought you extra napkins too, Brian.' She briefly placed a hand on his shoulder and left.

'Preferential treatment, I see. You must be a regular, or is she a friend?' The man's face remained focused on the spoon as he slowly rotated it in the cup.

'I call in most days when I can. This is where I usually get butter down my shirt.' He raised his eyebrows as he brought up the napkin and tucked it beneath his chin. 'Not very elegant but effective. Come here often did you ask? As I said, yes, but I've been a bit busy lately as we're—' He was going to say a member of staff down but stopped himself.

'She a friend?'

'No, she does most days and we've got to know each other.' Brian felt himself blush a little but could not understand why. 'Visiting Southport?'

'No, I live here.' He looked up for the first time. 'Well, can you believe, I live with my mother. I'm between apartments at present, relationship trouble, I'm afraid. I'm in car sales. Popped in to look at the beauty in the entrance. You probably know it belonged to Sir Henry Segrave.'

Carlos, with a mouth full of toasted teacake, shook his head. He, too, still lived at home. It seemed to be the malaise of his generation. What with job insecurity, house prices and, he had to admit, his inability to save. As Carla said, life is for living, and that meant spending and having a bloody good time.

'It's a Sunbeam Tiger and he drove that 152.33 miles per hour along the sands here. You have to admire his bravery. Ninety-four years ago, that is, according to the posters. Imagine travelling at that speed on sand with tyres like that. You're probably here for the same reason.'

Carlos could sense the enthusiasm as he spoke but his

ears pricked up on hearing the words 'relationship' and 'trouble'.

'No, just lunch. You know all of the figures and fine details. Who'd remember the point three-three in the story after so long?

'Been fascinated since I was a kid. My father was into design so cars like this featured heavily in my childhood. My brother was a designer at Jaguar too. Not cars, but the interiors. The subtle bits that make the difference, he used to say. I just flog them. It's my afternoon off so I thought I should come and pay homage to Sir Henry.'

'So that's why there's a pub and eatery called the Sir Henry Segrave? Do you know I never saw the connection until now and I've lived in Southport all my life too. Thought Sir Henry was some sort of politician!'

Carlos ate the remaining half of teacake and sipped his coffee. 'I'm sure I know you from somewhere.' He looked across, an inquisitive expression on his face.

'You ever bought a car?'

Brian shook his head screwing his eyes up. 'I haven't, but where have I seen you?'

'It's amazing how many people say that. They spend an hour with me in the showroom and I meet them six months later and they say "I know you."' He laughed and finished his coffee. 'Working in retail's like that. The girl who served you will tell you the same. You might possibly have seen me in the *Sir Henry*. I drink there often, more so now that I'm living at home. I'm sure we'd come to blows, mother and me, if I didn't get out of the house.' He laughed and raised his eyebrows. 'Must get a move on. I'll have another look around that beautiful old car and then home. I'll be popping along to the pub tonight for a meal, I think. The name's Lloyd.' He stood and came over proffering his hand.

'Brian, but people call me Carlos. Nice to meet you. And thanks for the history lesson. I'll know where to come when I need a car.'

'Indeed. If you fancy a drink and something to eat, I'll be in *Sir Henry* at about seven thirty.' The wink forced home the not-so-subtle inuendo.

Carlos blushed slightly when he said it. The fact that Lloyd's eyes lingered just a moment too long on his caused a shiver of excitement and brought a tingle. He had just been chatted up and he liked it. On leaving the table he went towards the girl behind the counter. He had a slight spring to his step. Smiling at the waitress he asked the question. 'Do people who come in here sometimes bump into you on the street and stop you, suggesting that they've seen you somewhere before?'

'All the time, Brian. They're not used to seeing me away from here and out of this outfit. One old dear thought I was her niece! Comes with the job.'

On leaving The Atkinson, the wind was driving the light rain in translucent sheets down Lord Street. He pulled up his hood and headed back to work.

Nicola greeted him. 'You seem to have had a good break?'

He smiled. 'Bloody weather! You might say that, it just might possibly have been profitable and that's all I'm saying.' His facial expression said it all. 'I'm all tongue tied!'

'Jim told me you found something you'd been looking for when you moved the furniture in the treatment room. Wasn't the twenty pound note I lost at Christmas was it?' She chuckled.

Carlos shook his head. 'No, just something and nothing, my notebook.'

Nicola's remark reminded him he needed to contact DI Decent as that would be the right thing to do. Although to him at the moment the majority of the contents of the book meant nothing, to the police they might prove to be vital. He took his phone and went to the treatment room. As he checked for the number, he heard the door and realised he had a client. It would have to wait until later.

CHAPTER 22

Tico's ears twitched as the key turned in the lock. Stretching his legs, he pulled himself up before arching his back. His tail, tucked and curled between his back legs, moved frantically, his usual excited greeting before launching himself at April as she walked into the hall.

'Missed me, Tico? Walk?'

There was no greater sign of enthusiasm but he headed immediately for the door. Grabbing his lead, she pulled on some wellington boots, an old coat and they left. The beach beckoned and the breeze and fresh sea air would blow away the confusion that had accumulated throughout the working day. Tico immediately relieved himself against a post, his post, as he did on most trips from the house. Soon he pulled out the lead to its fullest extent. Like April, he was glad to stretch his long legs.

Before leaving work, she had jotted down evidence from the case for Michael to chase up, attached to a note requesting miracles be done during the hours of darkness.

The photographs, the friends' lists and the latest intelligence were his on which to work his magic.

Noting there had been no response from the public concerning the appeal for details on the person seen in the background of the photographs, Michael turned to search the work carried out by Lynda's facial recognition unit. The approximate age of the individual had been established, alongside hair and skin colour. His task would be to dig further into the images of the party which had now been released.

* * *

Carlos had not given the notepad much consideration on leaving work. The idea of contacting the police had evaporated the more he thought about Lloyd and the possibility of a surprise meeting at the *Sir Henry*. He wondered if Lloyd suspected he would accept his invitation. He had showered and dressed before inspecting his appearance in the mirror. He checked his nails; as always, they were immaculate. '152.33 miles per hour for Sir Henry but our Lloyd's a fast worker too,' he addressed his reflection. For some reason the words 'decimal point' came to mind and along with it an extended flush of excitement.

The evening air and the darkening sky brought with it a chill once the heat of the day had left the streets. A light mist had crept in from the sea to take its place. It gave a magical, blurred look to the lights of the darkened town. Turning down Lord Street, there was still a red blush to part of the western sky; there were still gulls too, their nocturnal flight aided by the town's lights. It amazed him how the birds' moving shadows could startle when flying within the coloured spotlights, often placed to illuminate the various buildings. Southport had a beauty of its own, even though the residents were experiencing the recent, dark times. He thought of his mother who still checked to see if he had a clean handkerchief when he went out. 'You're still my little boy', she would always say, closely followed by, 'Do you have your key?' Although living at home had its drawbacks, it also had its advantages. He did very little, his food was bought and prepared, his washing and ironing done and even his bed made. To many he was spoiled but to Carlos he was cherished.

The pub stood out from the rest of the buildings in the row. Housed in a detached Victorian stone building, bedecked with central tower crowned with wrought iron, it had a certain regal presence. The blue surrounding iron and glass veranda that faced two sides was welcoming. The flower baskets hanging from the intricate iron work, trailing variegated ivy, were silhouetted against the pub's lights, making them look larger than life. Some seating was optimistically placed outside, and the wall heaters had attracted smokers and the hardy who congregated in groups.

Carlos paused, contemplating the significance of his chance conversation with Lloyd. It seemed an age since he had been drawn to someone after such a brief encounter. He had experienced carefree flings, spontaneous couplings he had called them, in a way to justify the feeling of disgust that often followed. He had promised himself, after a conversation with Carla, that those liaisons were to be a thing of the past. He promised her that he would respect himself more and from that moment he had. He recalled her words: 'You're worth more than that. Look after you. Look after number one as no bugger else will!' Her advice seemed to suggest that this was the guidance she had forced upon herself. She had faced toils and tribulations so often, brought about by Smith's frequent dalliances and disloyalty. These salutary experiences had changed her life. He felt himself growing maudlin. Crossing the road, he entered the building and directly approached the bar. The warmth, the music and the chatter were heady.

Campari and soda in a tall glass always looked inviting, and as the slice of orange floated to the surface to mix with the crushed ice, he stirred his drink. Lifting it up to the light he admired the colour, it was a rich and deep red. It was part of the drink's attraction, that and its bitter, herbal taste. He felt as though it cleansed his palate but that brought the words 'pretentious pomposity' to mind, and he giggled. When he had first ordered one in her company, Carla had made that comment to him. The words had stayed with him. Turning, he scanned the room before slipping the straw between his lips again. His eyes searched amongst the seated customers for Lloyd. On a table by the last window was the man for whom he searched. He smiled before waggling his fingers in recognition and moved over negotiating a number of customers and tables.

Lloyd stood and held out his hand. 'I didn't think you'd come, Carlos, or do you prefer Brian?'

'Carlos, I'd prefer. It brings a great friend and mentor to mind.' He sat looking at the dregs within his new found friend's glass. 'Another?'

'No, I need food. You okay with that?'

Carlos sipped from his straw and nodded as a menu was placed in front of him.

* * *

The pistol grip glass cutter followed the pattern clearly visible through the blue-green glass. April's steady hand pushed the wheel along a curved route drawn on the paper beneath the glass positioned on the light box. The fine cutting edge made a satisfying crunch as it scored the glass surface whilst leaving a light snail trail of fine oil in its wake. The distinctive sound told her that the pressure applied was accurate. On reaching the end she lifted the glass, rotating the cutter to bring the brass screw fitting on the chamber that held the cutting oil. She held it underneath before tapping it gently along the scored line. Obediently the glass broke perfectly. There was always something reassuring when a complex series of curving cut lines appeared from the full glass sheet. She had been taught well. Placing it onto the cartoon, the drawn black lined pattern of the design for the leaded window, she appreciated the richness of the colours she had chosen. She would cut one more before opening the wine. Checking her watch, her mind turned to Michael. He would just be getting to grips with the files she had left him.

* * *

Whether it was through excitement or a touch of nerves, Carlos did not finish his scampi and chips. He mauled his meal like a cat with a mouse. The conversation flowed; it was both easy and relaxed, as if they had known each other for longer. Within the matter of an hour, he had told most of his life story. There were, however, gaps deliberately left. Carla was never alluded to, even though at one point the conversation turned to discuss the three recent murders. It was Lloyd who had joked, somewhat tongue in cheek, that you waited years for a juicy murder to happen in your town and then three come along together. It had fallen flat, and that was the only time there was an uncomfortable pause in the conversation. However, on draining his third Campari soda, Carlos relaxed, enjoying the mood. The barriers began to be withdrawn and the mutual laughter was restored.

Looking out of the window, they saw that far more people had congregated around the tables and heaters. It was Lloyd who suggested they take a walk. 'I fancy a flutter on the penny slots!' His face beamed as he said it. '*Silcock's Funland* down by the pier, I need a bit of light relief in my life! Some gambling! Let's go wild and be free!'

Carlos laughed out loud. 'Penny, Lloyd? When did you last put anything less than ten pence in one of the slots at *Silcock's*?'

It brought a strange reaction from Lloyd who moved away, his expression changing immediately as he scowled.

Carlos, realising his words sounded rude and crude, tried to swallow them back as soon as he had uttered them. 'Sorry, that didn't come out like I meant it to, but you know what I mean.' He laughed hoping to bring the smile back to his new friend's face.

Lloyd laughed loudly. 'I know. How about we say, "in for a penny, in for a pound"?'

Carlos nodded and they set off down Coronation Walk.

Within minutes they approached the covered Gallopers Carousel standing outside the amusement hall; it was busy. Myriad lights sparkled and flashed, a siren to the carefree and the foolish. They stood and admired the painted carousel. The beautiful, colourful horses were still visible but were now trapped behind the steel mesh for the evening. Lloyd noticed the camera protruding from the amusement building roof that was focused just on the fairground ride. He turned and grabbed Carlos.

'Smile, you're on camera!' They both looked up, posing.

'Cheese,' Carlos responded before turning to point towards a bronze male figure atop a column, who looked as if he was about to dive into a pool. On closer inspection, he realised the diver had only one leg. He wore a helmet of sorts and an old-fashioned bathing suit. 'I've seen this statue so often but I've never studied it. One leg! See, I hadn't noticed that.'

'Let's not go in and gamble away our ill-gotten gains, let's just walk and I'll tell you all about this character.' Lloyd pointed to the diver. 'It might be apocryphal but you'll love the tale. What do you say?'

Carlos nodded his agreement. 'Apocryphal? Sorry but you've lost me already.'

Lloyd slipped an arm into the crook of his elbow and moved him along turning back the way they had come but dropping down towards the privacy of the lower promenade.

'Apocryphal, Carlos? Tonight, my friend, I might just be telling you a whole pack of lies!' He glanced sideways searching for a reaction but none was forthcoming. 'That man, my dear boy, is allegedly Professor Gadsby. Now what do you know about the one-legged pier divers?'

Carlos laughed out loud. 'Like the word apocryphal, I know absolutely nothing, but I feel I'm going to find out and have my leg pulled anytime soon.'

He had been listening but Lloyd wondered if at all he had been heeding.

* * *

April,

I hope your evening was as profitable as mine. I did enjoy the files but whether a miracle has been performed is for you to decide. If so, I shall expect to see an increase in my monthly salary! All has been updated.

You need to speak to Taylor and Gaskell about the parties held at the apartment. They both appear in the photographs but they were never at the same party. I've organised the pictures to show the different dates. When they were present, they seem to be chatting to many of the guests but I can't find one picture that includes both men. Secondly, when we do see them, both are observed using their phones as a camera and we've not requested those images. I've taken the liberty of submitting the request. To ensure co-operation, I've organised for officers to 'read', I think that's the terminology, their phones early tomorrow in the hope we can prevent the deletion of any content. We might be too late for that ... we'll see.

We also have our missing man; the one spotted at the back of the group shots taken around town. He's in one picture where we can see a clear side profile, and in some others too, but they're rear head shots. The hair, however, is of interest as it clearly shows signs of premature male patterned baldness. I'm aware some people have a skill of avoiding being captured on film, my wife has it. I feel that like her, he's such a person. However, that clearly contradicts the fact that he openly sat and watched photographs being taken of the group and I suggest he'd have known that his face would be captured. Whether he thought we would go to such lengths in analysing the images is another matter.

Finally, did some checking at Jaguar regarding Trevor Thomas. He resigned. He wasn't sacked. He'd had mental issues since his mother was diagnosed and found it hard to concentrate and then it was impossible for him to leave her. He became her part-time carer. He'd taken a good deal of leave on compassionate grounds by the time of her death. They had told him he was welcome to return to work when he could meet the demands of the job. I've attached the contact details of an Emma Barnes with whom I spoke last night.

I'll leave that with you.

Michael

CHAPTER 23

Walking away from the pier, the privacy and emptiness of the lower promenade suddenly became apparent and Brian suddenly felt vulnerable and frightened for the first time. He realised Lloyd had directed the whole evening and he had followed. For some strange reason the nursery rhyme flooded his mind: *'Would you walk into my parlour?' said the spider to the fly.* He stopped walking.

'Are you alright, Carlos? You've gone very quiet.'

His words were calm and reassuring. His smile diffused the sense of danger.

'I'm fine. I could kill a coffee.'

'You are dying for a coffee? So, coffee it will be. As we walk let me finish the tale. Our man on the pole was a pier diver. After the First World War there were a number of amputees. Some bright spark thought they could make a living by diving from the piers that were prevalent in the major seaside resorts such as New Brighton, Southport and Blackpool. There was no opportunity of their working as manual labourers so the bright ones looked at ways to make a living or supplement a wage. I read they would shout, "Don't forget the diver, don't forget the diver as every penny makes the water warmer!" Our man there was an academic. But when I did more research, I discovered that he didn't lose a leg in the war but was born with only one leg. Now, let's see if you are observant my dear Carlos. Get this right and you win a coffee. Which leg was missing on the diver?'

'The left one.'

'Correct. But when I saw a photograph taken in period of the man, Professor Gadsby, it showed that it was his right leg that was missing. So, is that Gadsby or not?'

'Are you making all this up?'

'Nope. Would I lie to you?' he did not wait for the reply. 'On a modern computer you can reverse a photograph and providing it doesn't contain writing it still looks genuine. To me, this is what happened with the old sepia picture, it was reversed or I like to believe it was. Whatever the case, he'll always be Gadsby the mono-pod diver to me. Now let's get you a coffee.'

Within minutes Lloyd had called a taxi.

'Why not get coffee on Lord Street?' Brian again felt uneasy. 'Why a taxi?'

'I live in Birkdale. I make great coffee and I have good music. Have the murders unnerved you? Could I be the killer stalking handsome young men and women?'

Brian looked at Lloyd and took a hesitant step backwards. 'I think I should just go home.'

'A killer who would meet his next victim in a public place where there are loads of cameras, walk with you to *Silcock's* which is bristling with cameras too? Stand by the statue that I feel sure is monitored and then get in a taxi that I have phoned for? That's an awful lot of incriminating evidence for the police to follow if they find you dead.' He stared at Brian and put his hands on his shoulders. 'I'm simply offering you a coffee. After that, I'll get you a taxi home.'

'And you live with your mother?' Brian replied. 'At least you told me you did or has that changed?'

'Unfortunately, yes, and her partner too. For the time being at least. However, things might soon change. Life has a way of creating new opportunities.'

The taxi pulled up by the war memorial. 'What's it to be. I can ask him to take you home or …'

Brian pondered for a moment and then smiled and nodded. 'Sorry, don't know what came over me, Lloyd. Coffee sounds perfect.'

Lloyd leaned over and gave the driver an address. 'Rotten Row, the junction with Weld Road.'

'It's only a couple of minutes by taxi but a pain in the arse to walk. You need your coffee too.' Lloyd smiled.

'Rotten Row, such a charming address.' Brian pulled a face.

It took three minutes. Brian climbed out leaving Lloyd to pay. 'Thanks, just live back there.' He pointed down the road as he smiled to the driver. 'This is fine.'

Lloyd waited until the taxi turned and headed back towards the town centre. 'My house is just around the corner. Needed some air. It's a couple of minutes from here.'

The house was large, detached, red-bricked and again Victorian. A light was on in the porch. Brian paused at the gates and looked at the scale of the place. The front garden had seen better days and so, too, had the house. It was showing its age and there was a general air of neglect.

'I know,' Lloyd laughed. 'Has a touch of the dramatic don't you think? Dracula's Castle comes to mind. Thought that as a kid and wouldn't venture either to the attic or the cellar. Always been a bit of a wimp. How are you, Brian, big and brave or are you like me, a bit of a coward when push comes to pull?'

'Never really thought about it much. Not good at school owing to being dyslexic. I've found my vocation now thanks to Ca—' He did not finish and left the sentence hanging.

He changed the subject back to the house. 'Most of the houses along here have been converted into apartments, nice ones too. Originally, when my parents were together that was their idea. My grandfather used to convert unwanted properties in the centre of town and my father worked with them. In the seventies few people neither wanted nor could afford to keep them, so they were converted either into apartments or businesses. When he left university, he took responsibility for the interior designing. He was good too, but then my parents split up. My father kept some in town and my mother got this after some wrangling over their split. My brother and I were left in the middle. Mind you, what was once a negative about the size of this place is now a positive as I have a section of the house to myself. We can be like ship's that pass in the night.'

The front of the house had a curved driveway comprising chippings that crunched beneath their feet. Grass grew in areas, predominantly where cars or feet had not trodden for some time. Brian paused again and looked at the house from the front. It reminded him of the type of house a child might draw. It was almost symmetrical with the door to the centre and two windows on either side. He thought of the small terraced home he shared with his mother. In consolation, his was the better maintained.

The entrance hall was expansive too, and a staircase ran to the right. They passed the mahogany, curved handrail when heading for a door at the far end. Lloyd opened it and showed Brian in whilst putting on the light.

'Take a seat. I'll add music and get the coffee. How do you like it?'

Brian looked around the room. It was well-designed, if not a little dated in his eyes and non too clean. His mother would not approve. The music, however, was perfect. He liked Snow Patrol.

Within minutes, Lloyd returned. 'Hope this is okay for you. I've brought a brandy too. I've enjoyed your company, Carlos. Let's hope we can do this again. It was good to chat. I've been under quite a bit of stress lately. A confidence thing. Possibly too friendly, that's my problem.'

'I don't think so.' Brian sipped the coffee. It was stronger and not as hot as he would normally take it but it was coffee, and he drank it quickly. Moments later he paused. Suddenly his head began to swirl. 'I've suddenly gone very dizzy, bloody Campari and soda coming back to haunt me,' he chuckled before falling back into the settee.

Lloyd sat and checked his watch. It should take less than ten minutes for the desired effect to take place. Brian's eyes closed. Standing, he went to the hall door and left the room for a moment returning with a wheel chair. 'Carlos, Carlos. Stand a minute. Let's get you on your feet and into some fresh air.'

Putting on the chair's brake, he moved and helped Brian to his feet. He swayed unsteadily, his eyes now intermittently opening and closing. His arms were by his side and a dribble of saliva ran from the corner of his mouth. Lloyd turned him whilst holding Brian's weight beneath his armpits before gradually lowering him onto the chair. He tossed a blanket over his legs. Brian was now just where he wanted him to be. In twenty minutes, he would be in the garage and there he would stay.

* * *

Gaskell looked at his watch as the intercom bell rang. He had just put bread into the toaster and poured his coffee. On hearing it was the police, he reluctantly released the door lock, turned off the toaster, and taking his coffee, went to wait and watch as the two officers ascended the stairs.

His smile was false as they took the last of the steps. One officer who seemed overweight and constantly wiping his brow, was carrying a small travel case.

'To what do I owe this early morning pleasure?' His sarcasm was direct.

The officers explained the reason for the call and informed Gaskell that they neither needed a warrant nor any other legal documentation to copy certain specified contents from his phone. They also pointed out that the process could be done at the station in Liverpool should he have any objections to co-operating in his own home. They handed him a pamphlet detailing his rights.

'Now?' Gaskell's voice had changed from being defensive as he showed them into the lounge area.

'It won't take long I can assure you. I believe you're in

possession of two phones, Mr Gaskell. Would that be correct?'

Gaskell's face flushed. *1984* came immediately to mind and that the monitoring state was more in evidence than he had imagined.

'I do, a business and a private one. Which do you need?'

'Both, sir, thank you.'

Whilst one officer observed Gaskell, the other unboxed the equipment he needed. The download time suggested forty-three minutes.

'What exactly are you taking from there without my consent?'

'Your contacts and your photographs including those stored within the cloud or any others linked digitally to external storage facilities. After that, we'll see.'

Gaskell returned to the kitchen and slammed the toaster back on. He had the face of a worried man.

CHAPTER 24

Skeeter was at her desk early even though she had run that morning. She watched as April walked through to her office. It took two minutes before she heard her name called. On entering, April was waving Michael's note.

'He was at one of the parties.'

'It's on file. Checking the system, it's all there, pics, the lot. The tech guys are at Gaskell's and Taylor's as we speak.' She paused as April continued to sort her desk, uncertain as to whether she was actually listening. 'Brian Briggs did not return home last night.'

'What?' She stopped immediately and looked directly at Skeeter.

'It's come straight through to us. His mother called this morning. He would normally ring if he were staying out overnight no matter what the time. He didn't. The recorded phone call suggests she only called us early because of the killings and the fact that Carla had gone missing before. I've requested CCTV for the area he was supposed to be in, and the surrounds. That should be coming in soon.'

Skeeter went around the desk and logged onto April's computer, bringing up the relevant file and recording of the call. They listened to the conversation. It had to be said Mrs Briggs was calm and controlled until the very end when she mentioned Carla. She told them what she knew of his plans for the evening.

'I want a member of the Family Liaison Team round there pronto. I also want both Rodgers and Sutch in here as soon as. Send a car, and I need the images from Gaskell and Taylor on this computer within the hour. Once you have finished get people into the Incident Room by nine.'

Skeeter moved quickly and went straight to Control, passing on a list of the requirements she had just received. 'Let me know a time for Sutch and Rodgers and call me when we have any CCTV footage.'

April called Mason explaining Briggs's disappearance and the planning she had put in place. She would have needed a sharp knife to cut the immediate silence.

'Get his photograph out there. All media channels now. High Risk disappearance. I'll be there as soon as.'

Skeeter's phone rang before she had reached the briefing. Sutch and Rodgers would be there within twenty minutes. There was also a message to say Nicola from the beauty salon had arrived at the front desk demanding Carlos be found; she was in an irate state. A WPC was with her. Skeeter made her way directly to try to calm the situation.

On seeing Skeeter, Nicola stood. She looked broken.

'His mother rang me. Is it true, and if so, what are you doing about it?'

Skeeter looked at the other officer and they both ushered Nicola to a seat.

'What do you know about yesterday's events? I want you to think of everything he might have said or done. Take a deep breath and concentrate. Right now, we need you calm and functioning. You might hold the vital clue we need to find Carlos.'

* * *

Although Skeeter received the call regarding the incoming CCTV, she redirected it. She spoke to Tony, her tone brisk. He soon switched on and linked the large interactive screen in the Incident Room to the recently sent file. The wonders of technology. The collected officers watched the edited footage.

'He's heading here towards the *Sir Henry*. Kasum, get onto the pub. I want all CCTV from last night. They'll send it directly so check it and stay until you have confirmation it's been sent. Emphasise the urgency.'

They continued to watch as Briggs crossed Lord Street. Kasum sidled from the room. Briggs's face was turned towards the camera positioned to focus down the street. The time and date were clearly marked at the corner of the images. The next frames showed him walking with another man towards *Silcock's Funland* and the pier, an area bristling with cameras. Those had already been collected and edited and they had produced a number of clear facial images of both men.

'We have a direct match for the guy who attended the party. If you check the rear view, he has the same balding area to the crown.'

Mason, leaning on one of the side walls, requested that

the film be paused. 'We need the best image we have, enhanced if at all possible, to accompany the one we have put out of Briggs. There's little point in watching more if we know the area where they were last seen on camera. We're wasting precious time, people. Neither man looks stressed, nor under threat. That could have changed. Let's find them and fast!'

Tony checked the notes. 'Last seen heading towards the entrance of Scarisbrick Avenue. No other sightings as yet but they're still looking. We can assume they might have got a lift from there.'

Mason smiled at Tony. 'We can make a calculated guess. Lucy, contact the local taxi companies. What time did we have them walking from *The Gallopers*? Check to see if anyone picked up two men in that area after.' He looked at Tony.

Tony slid the marker back to the point on the video. '10.17, sir.'

'We'll presume they met no one else. They either had a taxi ordered or telephoned for one. Describe them. No, hold on. Can we send a screen shot, Tony?' Mason looked inquisitively hoping for a positive response and smiled when Tony nodded.

Within seconds the shot was stored on file and referenced. He scribbled the reference number and handed it to Lucy. Control would put the calls out immediately, attaching the images to the companies' websites. They, in turn, would pass it on to their drivers or contract drivers. If they were working late, they might not pick the message up immediately.

* * *

The WPC placed a glass of water in front of Nicola.

'He'd gone out for lunch. He was late leaving. When he left he seemed so down. I could have cried for him. However, when he got back, he seemed like a different person. He was brighter and more positive.' She sipped the water and moved the tissue to her eyes. 'He was quite excited and certainly different from when he left.'

'Do you know why there was such a change in his mood?'

'No. He didn't come over to chat like I expected. He went to his treatment room. He waved and shouted that he'd forgotten to contact someone but didn't say who. Within a few minutes, his client arrived. Luckily, she was a little late, and Carlos came out straight away. I don't think he made the call after all.'

'Does he have a girlfriend or boyfriend he might have met up with?'

She shook her head. 'If he did, we'd have all known about it believe you me. He would readily talk about some of his past dalliances. They would make you blush, believe me.'

'Explain.'

'He used to be very carefree. You could say a bit too easy if you get my meaning. It was not good for him and certainly not good for his work. I nearly sacked him on a couple of occasions when he seemed to arrive here as if he'd just left someone's bed. Carla saved him really. She worked with him and gave him the guidance he needed. Many lads his age would have rebelled but he seemed to heed her advice. It was she who got him onto the straight and narrow. That's why the name – Carlos. He worshipped her.'

Skeeter immediately wondered if they were looking for one of those past partners, but then, why kill three people, both male and female? Why kill at all? 'Did the saying, the mantra, have anything to do with Carlos?'

She witnessed an immediate improvement in Nicola and a smile brushed her lips. 'We've just had the saying added to the wall of his treatment ro—' her voice trailed off thoughtfully and a puzzled look appeared on her face. 'When we were doing it, my partner and Carlos, that is, they moved the furniture. The room used to be Carla's as you know. It was then he found a notebook, a red one. He told Jim he'd been looking for it for ages. Now that I come to think about it, I remember seeing Carla with a small, red book.'

'Could it be the same one? Could that be why he wanted to call someone do you think? Is it still at the salon?'

Nicola spread her hands suggesting she was not sure. 'He could've taken it with him.' She removed her phone. 'Give me a minute.' She dialled, Jim.

'Hello love. No, nothing as yet. You remember the notebook you saw Carlos had when you were doing the mural thing in his room? Can you nip into the salon and see if it's there? Look in his treatment room, check the drawers. See if it's in the kitchen and search his locker, it's never locked. If it is, the combination is 0000. He was nothing if not original. Thanks. I'm still with the police. Ring me if you have it.'

'Thanks.' Skeeter put a hand on hers.

'It will take about thirty minutes. Is that okay?'

'Skeeter smiled. 'I'm going to have to leave you with Mary here. She'll let me know when you hear about the missing book. Believe me, we're doing everything possible to find him.'

* * *

Bill Rodgers and Debbie Sutch were ushered into the first Interview Room where DC Fred Quinn was arranging photographs on the table. Both looked flustered and uncomfortable. He welcomed them but did not manage to introduce himself fully before Sutch spoke.

'I know Brian, or Carlos, as they called him. Any news?' There was genuine anxiety trapped within the question. Her voice was shaky.

'Be assured we're working very hard to find him. We'd like you to look at these photographs but there's one in particular I'm interested in. This one.'

They sat and each looked at the same photograph. The image had been transposed from the CCTV as also had the one taken at the party.

'I've seen him before.' Debbie spoke first, lifting the photograph.

Fred watched, as she screwed up her face, as if trying to squeeze the answer out from every pore.

'I don't know his name but I remember him. God, yes! I do now. I trod on his foot accidentally when we were outside that pub down the side street near *The Scarisbrick*. You grabbed him and we all thought he was going to shit himself.' She looked at Bill who blushed, and glanced at Fred before nodding.

'I didn't hit him. I just grabbed him. I thought he'd deliberately crashed into Debs.' Rodgers protested his innocence guiltily.

Fred raised his eyebrows, aware of the case notes from his previous conviction.

'I've seen him a couple of times since, he's usually on his own. Sad fella really.'

'And you didn't hit him? There was no altercation at all?' Fred looked between the two of them.

'Definitely not. I just grabbed him.'

'And I stood between them and pushed this fella away. I could sense the guy's fear and I could also see Bill's anger. Since his conviction he listens to me. The rest of the group would just goad him to self-destruct. He's quite capable of that if he's had too many, be a real daft sod.'

Rodgers looked at his hands, his head nodding in agreement.

'Who was there on that occasion? Can you remember?'

It was upon hearing this question that something struck them both. Debbie's hand moved across to cover Bill's, and her other went to her mouth. 'Oh Christ!'

* * *

Skeeter hurried back to the room in which Nicola was waiting. On arrival she saw a man she presumed to be Jim standing by her. In her hand was the notebook. She waved it with a look of relief on her face.

'It was in the same place where he'd found it, beneath the bottom drawer. He'd taped it. It's definitely Carla's. I remember seeing it.' She handed it to Skeeter. 'It's her writing and those are definitely her doodles. She was always scribbling, especially when she was on the phone to clients.'

Turning the page, Skeeter immediately saw the doodles. She flicked the next page slowly and narrowed her eyes as if trying to see if the squiggles were significant. Turning another page, she then saw the first initials, dates and number. She continued. Moving to the white board she jotted down the details in the order in which they appeared within the book. CJ, FL, CG, BR and PW. She then circled the initials CJ, wrote Cameron Jennings, and linked it with an arrow.

'Any other ideas?' She looked at Nicola.

'BR could well be Bill Rodgers. He was a past boyfriend and she was still seeing him before she died.'

Skeeter added a circle around the initials CG, and wrote the name Craufurd Gaskell before turning to look at them both. 'Know him?'

'He owned the flat Carla and Callum rented on Lord Street, I think. Strange name, that's why I remember it.'

'Correct. What of the others?'

Both turned to look at each other but then shook their heads almost in unison.

'Just a minute!' Skeeter left the room returning a few minutes later with a photograph of Craufurd. 'Is this him?' She tapped the board by his name.

'Yes. I saw him a couple of times at their parties. We didn't go to every one but I remember Carla saying that he refused to go to them all, something about looking after the other tenants' interests whatever that meant. Compromised his landlord status.'

Skeeter looked back at the board and then her focus returned to Nicola and Jim. 'You've been most helpful. Thank you. We'll hang on to this and keep you informed over the coming few days.' Skeeter prepared to leave. They both appeared a little shocked. 'We'll find him.'

They stood, turning to leave. Jim slipped his arm around

her shoulders as Skeeter let her fingers flick again through the pages. 'Nicola, one last thing. The private evening work you both did, one night a week, I was told. What was it?'

There was no look of surprise on Nicola's face as she turned back. 'Friends, people who couldn't get in during the day or needed something special. These things help make the wheels go round in our industry. People always want to feel special and as a salon we help to fulfil that.'

'Doing what?'

'Nails, that's my thing. They can be intricate, and if you are going to a special event you do them as late as possible.'

'And Carla, what did she offer?'

'What nobody else could. CACI treatment. It was her thing.'

'Thanks. As I say, we'll keep you fully informed.'

She knew that the chance of their locating a body was far more likely than finding Carlos alive. They too would be very much aware of that. Now she needed to identify the two missing characters from the notebook.

CHAPTER 25

April was perching on a desk in the Incident Room, in conversation with Mason. Skeeter dropped the notebook onto the desk and tapped it with her finger. Both Mason and April turned to look.

'Found by Briggs in what was Carla's treatment room. If you recall she did foreigners one night a week, as did Nicola. Supposedly it's some new-fangled beauty treatment, and she was teaching Briggs the techniques. This little book might just shed more light on the type of treatment she was providing or selling. Nicola had an evening too, but she worked on nails so I doubt many men came in for that.'

Mason turned to look at her. 'Sex?'

'Study the initials. I'll leave you to draw your own conclusions.' Skeeter grinned.

'Bill Rodgers, Cameron Jennings, possibly, and could that be Gaskell, the flat owner?' April scanned the board until she located his name. 'Craufurd?'

'Just two to go to win the speed boat.' Skeeter mimicked a popular television presenter.

Mason laughed. 'Didn't think you were old enough, Warlock.'

Kasum moved across to the group. 'We have positive IDs on both from the *Sir Henry*. They ate there last night. Paid cash. One of the staff believes she's seen both of them before, but not together. One, she thinks, is called Frank, but she was not one hundred percent certain.'

April let her fingers open the page showing the initials FL.

'That's not all,' Kasum continued. 'We have a contact from Coastline Taxis. One of their drivers picked up two men at the entrance to Scarisbrick Avenue at about ten fifteen last night. He recalls one was Carl, but that's all he can remember. Dropped them at the end of Rotten Row. There was no specific address. The driver said the one who paid told him he lived just down the road.'

'The name Carl could easily be confused with Carlos. You wouldn't always match a short English chap with the name, Carlos.' She nodded at Kasum. 'Thanks, Kasum. Go with Skeeter. You're going to bring in Craufurd Gaskell. There's to be no ifs or buts. He'll not argue with either of you, I feel sure. Arrest him if he does and caution him.'

'For what?' Kasum asked, uncertain if a crime had been committed.

'Obstructing the police in the line of their enquiries ... Christ! Make something up!'

* * *

Simon Taylor answered his phone; he could see the call was from Craufurd.

'Did you get contacted by the coppers this morning at some God forsaken time?' The voice was tinged with anger and a hint of fear.

'Indeed, Craufurd, and to make matters worse, they raped my bloody phone before my very eyes. Told me it was fucking legal. I could hear the poor thing protesting. You, too, from the panic in your voice. Still have the sordid movies, do we?'

There was silence from the other end of the phone but he could hear the intake of breath. 'Well?'

'Fortunately, no. Transferred them on your sound advice. They're on separate memory sticks here in the flat but they won't be after today.'

'Those sordid movies of you and Carla. Taking advantage of a drunk. You should be ashamed. You're old enough to be her father!'

'I'm not, and she consented on most occasions. Besides, the mistake was showing you!' Craufurd snapped defensively.

'You had to after I found the hidden spy camera secreted in what was their bedroom linked to your phone. I could have ruined you and taken you to the cleaners, man.'

There was silence. 'It was off when you moved in and I unfortunately forgot to remove it. I made a mistake. That's what jealousy and infatuation does to a man of my age as you should know. Besides, you received compensation for the error in the form of rent-free accommodation for the duration. Let's come back to today's intrusion. I was informed that the person committing the murders was supposedly at one or more of the parties held here in the flat. They've added a picture of the guy who's gone missing and the killer, although they don't refer to him as that. However, they've asked the public not to approach them but to call 999 if they see either. I don't recognise him. Take a look. Ring me if you do.'

'Maybe he was on one of your videos?'

Craufurd quickly hung up.

* * *

The Incident Room was buzzing with activity. The photographs received from both Taylor and Gaskell were being filtered and the relevant images taken at the parties were being processed. It was during this procedure that an mp4 was located. It was the only one. It stood out like a sore thumb within the files. To those officers trained in IT investigation, this proved unusual. Considering most people have a phone that will shoot video, many store them within their files. They were usually street incidents or concerts. The eight-minute movie was immediately dispatched to April. Discarding what she was doing she opened the file and watched. It showed Carla lying on the settee in what she presumed was Gaskell's apartment. She was naked and appeared to be asleep. Moments later Gaskell appeared. He too was naked.

* * *

Brian sat on the chair to the back of the garage, the same chair to which Carla had been taped. Silver gaffer tape secured his arms and his legs; a knotted rag filled his mouth.

Lloyd had to admit that from a distance, and in the hazy light, it could well have been Carla.

'Do you recognise the car? You saw Carla in it when you were running. I noticed you, in fact, she pointed you out. The police have been looking for it. In the trade see, work with number plates, trade plates, cars. That bit was easy.'

The same dim light filtered into the room through the wired glass window set high in the wall. Carlos struggled against the tape that bound him and his guttural grunts conveyed a blend of anger and fear.

'Why do people get into cars with their killer is the question that's going through your mind right now? Carla did. She hesitated for a moment but then got in. Jennings did. He climbed out of his and into mine. The only one who hasn't so far is Groves. He stayed in his own. He drove himself to our rendezvous, the carpark and that saved me a job. I have one more to persuade, just one. The toughest nut to crack is yet to come but now there's you, Carlos. Where were we? Getting into vehicles with a stranger. You climbed into a taxi with me. Yes, you very nearly didn't but in the end you did. Carla was the same. She was uncertain but when I told her that Nicola had had been in an accident and she had directed me to her, she was quick to get in the car. For you it was the thought of sex, for Jennings too. You won't believe me, Carlos, but I'm truly sorry for all of this. It wasn't my fault. I didn't start it. It was Carla and her crowd and that bully she was meeting, Bill Rodgers. They all started it and there was no justification. I promised myself that I would always seek retribution when I experienced injustice, and I have. Years ago, when I was a timid youth, I had a poster on my wall of Jean-Claude Van Damme. Although I realised I couldn't be like him, I could, using other means and methods, seek and gain revenge. Some of those present have been labelled and dealt with. See.'

From a bench, he collected a book containing their photographs taken throughout their ordeal. 'Look, it's Carla, your dear Carla. She was the first, the one who goaded Bill on. She wanted him to fight with me, hurt me. I could see that. I also believed she knew who I was, and just like on the previous occasion when we'd met, she lacked all human kindness. Yes, you'll tell me she was drunk and not like that at all. She was good to you, I know that, but she harboured a secret and she could be cruel. Did you realise that?'

Lloyd could see the confusion written large across the younger man's face.

'She was a whore and a cruel one at that. Look!' He removed the book containing the photographs. 'Here she is just before she died. You don't think that's her, do you? She's hidden behind the goggles but that's her. She was crying. It is Carla, trust me. See, here's a photograph of her face.'

Carlos closed his eyes, refusing to look.

'Open them and look or I'll remove your eyelids with these.'

He picked up a pair of scissors and ran them across the back of his hand. Carlos felt the cold metal and it had the desired effect. He stared at the images and then looked back at Lloyd. Whatever he was trying to say was absorbed by the knotted cloth and came out as separate grunts.

'Remember when we met at the Atkinson and we talked cars? You asked about the speed and why point three-three was relevant. Remember that conversation, Carlos?'

He nodded.

'Well, I timed how long it took them to die. Just like they timed Segrave. From the moment the blade entered their flesh to their last gasp. The decimal point is critical, believe me. Amazingly, there was very little difference.'

Lloyd watched the tiny hemispheres of sweat bead the man's forehead, even though the temperature in the garage was low. Some collected enough perspiration to begin to roll down the side of his face. He leaned across and wiped away those remaining with the edge of the scissors.

'Fear does that to people. You're no different.'

He stood, moved across to a cardboard box on the far side of the garage and selected a piece of Carla's clothing.

'Smell, Carlos. Do you recognise the scent?'

Carlos thrust his head back. Tears flooded his eyes before cascading like the sweat down his cheeks to collect in the rag wrapped round his face. He struggled again.

'Now, where was I? Jennings, yes, he too. He could have stopped it but my belief is that he's also frightened of Bully Bill. He was also easy to snare …'

CHAPTER 26

Gaskell followed Skeeter into the Interview Room recently vacated by Sutch and Rodgers, and was shown to one of the chairs. She had called ahead and April was ready for them. A laptop was positioned on the table as was a number of photographs.

'Take a seat. May I remind you that you've been cautioned and that this interview will be recorded. Your rights are on that paper in front of you. I do suggest you read it, and we'll answer any questions you might have.'

April swiftly had a quiet word with Skeeter who raised her eyebrows.

'Mr Gaskell, my name is DI Decent and, yes, before you ask, I'm decent by name and decent by nature. Thank you for your co-operation.'

He was about to protest but then thought better of it.

'As you're aware, we've been investigating not only the death of your previous tenant but also the murder of two of her friends within the group. Another member has now gone missing. From looking through photographs taken at the parties held at the apartment they rented, we've found a match for the person for whom we are searching. We've also gone through those taken from your phone. This is the person.'

She slid the image across the table.

'What can you tell me about him?'

Gaskell studied the photograph and then looked back at April. She could see surprise on his face as he returned his gaze to the man. 'No, sorry. There were many people there I didn't know. I just took a few photographs. I was aiming at nobody in particular.'

April leaned across and collected it before opening the laptop. She found the edited CCTV footage of the night Carlos was caught on CCTV with the man in question and turned it towards Gaskell. 'This, Mr Gaskell, is footage of the same man taken last night. Please take your time.'

'I've just told you; I don't know him. What's wrong with you people? Would you prefer it if I told you that I recognise him but I don't know his name?'

April held up her hand to stop his protest before retrieving the laptop. She moved the track pad and found the next file. Starting it, she turned the screen to face Gaskell.

As the video started, Skeeter and April paid particular attention to Gaskell's face. Within a minute he looked at both officers. 'Where the fuck did you get that?'

'Your telephone records. Would you like to tell us about this? From what our experts report, it clearly constitutes rape. Carla Sharpe is certainly not in a position to give her consent.'

The silence was deep, thick and viscous. Neither side seemed to want to penetrate its surface.

* * *

'Jennings was so concerned for Carla, he rushed to help. He got into that very same car. There was some reluctance but I repeated the same to him, that Carla had once said to me when I couldn't, "Just do it!" Those were always her words and so they've stuck in my mind ever since. I was with her on the treatment table and when she said it, I was so angry. Comes from Nike, you know that of course, but do you know who the real Nike is?'

He moved within inches of Carlos's face. 'The winged goddess of Victory, speed and strength. I became that winged person seeking out revenge. At school it was easy. It was subtle. Their bike would go missing, their clothing after PE. Little things, you might say, childish acts, but each mattered to me. Each deserved a tick on my wall … a swoosh!' He placed the point of the scissors on Carlos's forehead and traced the mark of a tick. He applied enough pressure to compensate for the instinctive jerking of his head, a backwards movement in an attempt to avoid the weapon. Blood soon beaded from the cut and quickly diluted with the salty sweat.

As the pain seared through him, Carlos realised that the man he had spent his lunch with, the man with whom he had shared his evening meal, a drink and had a laugh with was not now the same man. Fear forced his bottom lip to tremble and as his knees bounced, more tears appeared.

'Did you know the name Nicola comes from the name Nike? Strange, the coincidences in this life we live.' He wiped the blood from his head with the item of Carla's clothing and tossed it on the floor.

* * *

'Let me tell you something else. We'll have a warrant to search your property, Mr Gaskell, whilst you are held here under arrest. It's being organised as I speak. That will allow the removal of any other computers, electronic tablets and items of electronic storage we might find. When you've been an officer for some years you are never surprised by how many old phones or SIM cards people keep. To cap all of that, we'll even organise a solicitor for you, unless of course you would prefer to get your own. This situation might not have been necessary if we'd had your full co-operation from the start. We're going to call on your ex-wife and chat to her. Stirs the mud from the bottom of a clear pond all of this, don't you think? Hiding facts always makes the water so murky, we can rarely see the truth.'

'I did not take that photograph on my phone. It is at the apartment; I do recognise my own interiors but I didn't take that.'

Neither April nor Skeeter spoke and the silence again grew thick. April began to allow her fingers to beat a rhythm on the tabletop. It was soft and in a way soporific.

'It's my son,' Gaskell mumbled.

Skeeter looked at April.

'Say that again.'

He's my son, and I'm sure you're barking up the wrong bloody tree. He's not a killer.'

'When did you last see your son?' April had stopped drumming, her concentration now focused directly on him.

'It's hard to believe, we both live here in Southport but I haven't seen him for five years, maybe more. You lose track.'

'We're all ears.'

* * *

Lloyd regarded Carlos as his head lay to the right. The blood had stopped from the scratch made by the scissors' point.

'I'm not going to kill you, Carlos. You've done me no harm. Unless of course, you don't do as you're told. In a strange way, I've come to like you. I admire the loyalty you've demonstrated to Carla and your boss. So why are you here? I hear you ask yourself in that confused brain of yours. You're here, Brian, as bait. You're my sprat to catch a bully mackerel.'

Carlos started to move and squirm within the chair. The look in his eyes suggested one thing to Lloyd, he needed the toilet.

'Toilet?'

Carlos nodded frantically.

'You can't. It must stay here. Sorry, Carlos.'

Lloyd watched as the dark stain flushed the front of his trousers and then ran down each leg before pooling by either shoe. He watched the tears run, too, as Carlos strained against the tape.

'Sorry. You must believe me, how sorry I am. If this works and I have them all then you'll be free and that,' he pointed to the puddles, 'is but a small price to pay.'

CHAPTER 27

Gaskell fumbled with his fingers, his nerves clearly beginning to show before he looked directly at April. 'His mother and I were never married. He was illegitimate but to me an unnecessary bastard. In my opinion neither of us was ready to have kids. I had too much living to do, a business to build, if the truth be known. We split early on and to save complications, after some wrangling, I gave her the house. I didn't want anything to do with them. She was pregnant, too, but it may well not have been mine – her proclivity to like the company of the opposite sex was one of the reasons we split. I suppose I'd no right to expect her loyalty, as I'd never truly commit to the relationship, I wouldn't propose, even when Frank was born. There were so many couples at the time deciding not to tie the knot. Probably the start of how things are today. I even resented the boy. I wanted her to terminate. We weren't short of money and that certainly wasn't an issue.'

'Frank?' Skeeter asked, checking the name of the person on file.

'Frank Lloyd. I pushed for that. If we had to have a child then I wanted the opportunity to name him. Influenced by my love of my job in a way – a man I admired – Frank Lloyd Wright. People think he was just an architect, but he was more than that, in fact he was a brilliant interior designer.'

'What's your son's full name, Mr Gaskell? We need a phone number and an address too, urgently.'

'Frank Lloyd Millington. No idea about his phone but ...' He added the address.

April looked at the camera knowing the conversation was relayed to the Incident Room and that the required action would be immediately co-ordinated and sanctioned.

'Is your son a potential killer?'

Gaskell shrugged his shoulders but there was clearly uncertainty in the action. 'I pay certain bills, or I did until he reached twenty-one. I sincerely hope not but these days with so many drugs available, you just never can tell what ways their minds might be warped.'

* * *

The address was located and Mason organised the key Matrix teams to readiness – firearms, drone and the chief negotiator were all primed. A time was set for the move on the property and local pre-ordered plans utilised to direct the close operations. There was a procedure for the readiness of street closure when dealing with a major incident and the emergency services were readied. Decent and Warlock vacated the Interview Room leaving Gaskell in a state of confusion. The officer remaining was briefed to ensure a duty solicitor was contacted.

'You'll be staying here for a while longer until we discover just what other evidence we find during the search. Make yourself comfortable.'

The briefing was just that, brief. The Incident Room was busy. A Street View image of the house situated on Parkside Road was visible, projected onto the large screen to the far end of the room. Within twenty minutes they would receive live drone images of the location, concentrating on the garden area. The height and distance of the machine would be such as not to attract unnecessary attention at the house.

'April and Wicca, I want you on the ground. April, you will maintain your role as SIO. Firearms and a negotiator will be on standby along the Oxford Road end of Westbourne Road, with medical and fire and rescue support if it's required.' Mason pointed to the area. 'The properties along these two roads have huge rear gardens, what they contain will only be ascertained once we have aerial images coming in live. We'll be using thermal imaging too. You will co-ordinate target entry point and time of entry once the intelligence has been received and assessed here. Communication will be standard: Gold, Silver and Bronze. The Incident Room will continue as Gold and those on the ground as Silver, all others will communicate as Bronze. The Major Incident Vehicle will be there on your arrival. I'll keep you up to speed whilst you're travelling. We've isolated an area of the golf links' carpark for the drone operation. It's away from the public eye and hopefully the Press's nose. That will provide us with a short time operating range. Local area Traffic Officers have been notified.'

The patrol car blocked the narrow road after the marked transit moved into position. Within a matter of minutes, the landing area was coned and the police drone made ready. Live stream images would be linked with communications from the officers on the ground. Each officer was identified by an electronic tag which would show up on screen. Having the silent eye in the sky, with its multiple cameras, would enhance the track and trace of all in the designated area.

Skeeter drove. The flashing strobes, normally concealed within the grille and the headlights, ensured swift movement along the busy roads. April continued to monitor the progress of the team arrivals.

'The drone's up and we have live images here.' April briefly flicked the electronic tablet sideways before turning it back. Skeeter paid no attention. Her concentration was on the road. Her growing frustration became a constant diatribe aimed at motorists who seemed unaware they had purchased a rear-view mirror when they bought the car. It was a constant commentary.

As the drone hovered above the targeted area, there was nothing coming up on thermal imagery from the garden to either the front or rear of the address. The officers' identification tags were clearly visible but as yet there was nothing positive on the suspect.

CHAPTER 28

Lloyd brought two cans of coke from a box on the bench placing a straw in one. 'I bet you're thirsty. I know I am. I'm going to trust you. I'll remove the cloth from your mouth and release one hand. It's my act of kindness to you, but I need your promise. Should you call out or try to move, I will simply kill you.' He removed a sheathed craft knife from his pocket. 'It would take a minute for me to perform that cruel act and a few minutes for you to die, probably three for it all to be over. We'll not think about the seconds for the moment. The truth is, Carlos, after Jennings, I wanted to be caught.' Lloyd held out a can and Carlos drank quickly before choking. Coke came down his nose as he tried to find his breath. Lloyd tapped his back gently. 'Steady, no one will take it away from you. Take your time. If you're good then you'll have a lifetime. Where was I?'

'After Jennings you …' Carlos answered. It was uttered almost in a whisper.

'Yes, thank you. I find it hard to concentrate for long periods these days, possibly the guilt or the fear of what's to

238

come. Something inside of me often screams that what I'm doing is wrong, possibly evil. In a way, I think it's as cowardly as the first incident involving Rodgers and his bully boy actions. I know, now, I've become the aggressor, the tormentor and, I suppose, the destroyer. It's taken neither strength nor speed. Yes, it's taken a degree of courage, but that's because I didn't face the people directly; it wasn't a confrontation. I faced them when their guard was down and they were at their most vulnerable. Vulnerable, Carlos, that's like me.' He drank from his can before wiping his mouth on his sleeve. 'That's how I've been all my life! I wanted them to find me, the police, and put a stop to it. I left clues, the shoes, the caps, the DVDs. You see the coppers in television programmes and they suddenly spot something at the crime scene. They swing into action and catch the killer before more harm is done. When we were out last night, we passed so many CCTV cameras. I knew they were there; I'd planned the route. But are they looking? Have they identified me? It's all slowing down, Carlos. In my head it's slowing.'

Carlos shook the can and angled it to suck out the remnants. He was more interested in the coke than the ramblings of the man in front of him.

'Remember the carousel?'

Carlos nodded, keeping the straw between his lips. His mouth still seemed so dry; the cool liquid had tasted like nectar.

'When I was young, my mother took us to the merry-go-round. I don't know whether it was the strange music these machines played, you know, that organ sound.' He played the imaginary keyboard with the fingers of one hand as he spoke. 'Or the other children's screams of excitement, or was it possibly fear? The horses' wild faces, all flaring nostrils, teeth and wide staring eyes, or was it something else? I was never quite sure. Later in life I discovered the truth, I found my phobia. It was none of those things. It was the speed of the carousel's rotation. As a very young child I had night-mares. There were neither clowns nor carousels involved but a conveyor belt running at a set speed. It never changed for what seemed like hours, it was constant. On and on it went, almost hypnotic and mesmerising but also disturbing. I'd wake up soaking wet and screaming. From then on, when-ever I see something travelling at that actual speed, I grow anxious and scared. What's strange, Carlos, when I get frightened everything slows to that speed, voices, music, people. It's as if everything around me becomes synchro-nised to that terrifying pace. Do you think I'm slightly crazy, maybe even a little mad? Am I going insane, do you think?' He threw his can hard against the wall and a stream of dark liquid and froth sprayed in an arching fan-like cascade before the can clattered and settled on the floor. It spun momentarily, driven by the escaping fluid. 'Do you?'

Carlos stared at Lloyd, uncertain as to how he should respond. His heart wanted to scream *you're a fucking murdering lunatic* as loudly as his lungs would allow but he shook his head in response. 'No, I think you've been hurt too much in your life. Although I feel sure you've experienced a mother's love, you've not had the love and attention of your real father. I had, until my father passed away; I valued that love. I went off the rails when he died, but I was helped and cherished by those around me. You've not met those who would cherish you.' Carlos could hear the tremble in his own voice and feel the quivering of his lower lip.

'Girls? I tried with girls you know, but I could never perform. That was one of the problems with Carla. Just couldn't do it. Christ, even when it was on a plate. She was unkind too then. "Just do it, for goodness' sake". Those were her exact words. At that moment, for me it was impossible. It was her eyes. Everything slowed down and I left, tail between my legs, you might say. I bet she told them all, and that's why they all laughed on that fateful night. They knew my secret and they laughed.' A false smile cracked his lips, but Carlos could sense the sheer resentment the incident had sown. 'They're not laughing now, though. Every cloud as they say.'

Carlos suddenly recalled the notebook he had found and he thought of the initials FL followed by the zero. 'Do you have another name, Lloyd?'

Lloyd laughed. 'Frank Lloyd Millington. I should have been a Gaskell but if I had my way, I'd be simply Lloyd.' There was a moment's pause. 'Enough of this bullshit.'

Leaning over he snatched the coke can from Carlos's hand leaving the straw dangling between his lips. He quickly removed it, replacing the gag and strapping his arm back to the chair.

'I don't know how to love, but I know how to hate.'

Within minutes Carlos heard the side door open and then close, the key turn in the lock and then all was silent.

* * *

April and Skeeter climbed the steps before entering the Major Incident Mobile Unit. Blue-and-yellow fluorescent chequering ran down either side; an awning from the roof hung over the now closed footpath. Three further police vehicles were parked behind, followed by an ambulance. April recognised Max Foster immediately, senior firearms officer and DI Peter Jones, one of the Crisis and Hostage negotiators; he was a highly trained police officer with many years' experience.

'We have a man on the ground on both parallel streets. Another is in position at the top of Parkside Road and one at the bottom. So far there's been no activity. The property is occupied by a Mrs Margaret Millington and her son Frank Lloyd. The other son works down south and as far as we're aware is still there. We're trying to contact him. According to a neighbour, there's also a long-term partner living in the house but he works on a Saturday in Liverpool and should be there at the moment. Again, we're trying to make contact.'

Checking her watch April adjusted the time to match the digital clock within the unit. 'We'll go on the hour. Standard procedure for this one with your guys taking the lead. Front, rear and garden in one co-ordinated move. Once clear in all areas we will follow.'

Gold and Bronze were notified of the orders and further instructions were sent. Steve was ready along with the drone. His role was critical in monitoring the movements of friend and foe in the area of the house, a technique for which he had trained. He checked his watch before making final positional adjustments of the hovering drone in readiness.

The vehicles began to move. Once parked and in position the command to move would be given. Tensions always ran high at this juncture. Skeeter and April pulled on protective vests and high visibility jackets clearly marked with the word 'Police'.

CHAPTER 29

L loyd checked his phone. Rodgers should be at home but if not, he would wait. He slipped on a pair of glasses.

Bill Rodgers had just finished showering when his doorbell rang. He grabbed a dressing gown and pressed the intercom.

'Mr Rodgers? Merseyside Police. Sorry to disturb you so early on a Saturday but we have some information regarding Debbie Sutch. I believe she's a friend of yours. We need your assistance urgently.'

He had not finished the sentence when the lock clicked and the door opened slightly.

'Come up. Second on the left.' There was a slight shake to Rodgers's voice.

Rodgers grabbed a towel and began rubbing his hair as the knock came on the door he had deliberately left ajar.

'Thanks, sir. DC Frank Lloyd. Sorry, as I said …'

Rodgers stopped drying his hair and stared directly at the man entering. 'Have we met before?' Bill moved closer.

'You came to the station, about the murders? I think we met briefly then.' Frank Lloyd was making a huge assumption. Luckily it seemed to work in his favour.

Rodgers backed off.

'However, we also met before, socially. We met just outside a pub off Lord Street, way before all of this murder and mayhem started. Debbie, your kind partner, stepped backwards and bumped into me. You and the rest of your now-diminished group thought it highly amusing – Cameron Jennings, Carla Sharpe and not forgetting poor old, Stuart Groves. All gone.' He ran his finger across his throat. 'As easily as that!'

Rodgers pulled a face. 'What the fuck are you talking about?' His aggression was clearly evident on his face.

'I'm not a police officer, I'm a salesman, and I'm good at my job.' He removed his glasses and tucked them into his pocket. 'People believe me. I can sell sand in the desert.' He paused and pushed the door closed with the back of his shoe. 'I hate bullies. I've always been bullied, ever since I was a kid and I vowed that even though I can't fight I can retaliate in other ways.'

Rodgers threw down the towel and moved towards the man, his fists formed and his face reddening.

'Stop! Let's think of Debbie Sutch. You really don't want to upset or hurt me. That would be good for no one at this moment, least of all you. Right now, you're responsible for the deaths of those people you called friends. You might even be responsible for one more death if you lay one, small finger on me today.'

The bizarre circumstances in which Rodgers found himself were clearly confusing. The idea that a police officer was suggesting that he was responsible for the deaths did not make any sense at all. 'Where's Debbie?'

'Safe. Let's sit like two sensible adults and talk this through. I killed them, all of them, starting with Carla. I hold up my hands – mea culpa, Mr Rodgers, mea culpa. But then, you forced me to do it so you were the one who metaphorically pulled the trigger. I simply held the gun.'

'What the fuck are you on about! Are you for fucking real?'

Frank Lloyd remained calm even though he felt his heart could be seen pounding in his chest. He sat casually and waved his hand for Rodgers to follow. 'No? You don't want to listen to reason? Then I'll leave and that will be it.'

'You won't leave here. I'll fucking beat you bloody senseless, to a fucking pulp and then get the police.'

'And then, you say correctly because *and then.*' He emphasised each syllable. 'Another life will be taken … an innocent life. I'll never divulge where the person is hidden, neither to you nor the police. They will die eventually, locked away with no food, no water. A slow and dare I say it, if all deaths are not deemed to be cruel, a cruel way to die. All because of you!' He pointed his finger. 'Your friends need you now to act for them but not in your role as bully. They need you to be selfless! Mr Rodgers, nobody will ever make me reveal the person's whereabouts. In the past, like now, I was frightened of you but at the moment this no longer applies. You see, the difference is, death no longer worries me. I've seen it, smelled it and, yes, it has a particular odour. In my mind I've flown over it like a winged god destroying to create. Destroying, Mr Rodgers, so that I can create this very window of opportunity to be with you.'

'If anyone's going to fucking kill anyone it will be me kicking you down those fucking stairs. You fucking nutter.'

'Think for a moment of someone else and not yourself. You, Mr Rodgers need to listen and I need to speak. Is that understood?'

Rodgers paused and looked directly into the man's eyes. They were empty. There was neither emotion nor a flicker of any feelings; they were as dead as those named within the group. He sat.

* * *

Skeeter could hear the sound of the drone to her left. It seemed a long way off but she knew its capabilities.

'Nike is riding high.' Turning, she glanced at the screen April held which showed a clear view of the house from the air. She could also count the heat register from each of the numbered officers on the ground. She watched them disperse to their designated positions.

'They go in three,' April announced, as the final armed officers moved to the front door. One of the rapid entry team carrying the ram they liked to refer to as the 'master key', moved into position in readiness to break through the door. If Carlos was held in the building, the element of surprise gave him a greater chance of survival.

The sound of splintering wood and breaking glass was immediate. The multiple yells of the fast-moving officers as they entered followed swiftly on. Skeeter could hear the challenges – 'Armed Police' followed by the announcements, 'Clear' – as each room was searched. The process was rapid and efficient. April and Skeeter moved quickly once the building was secured and they had received clearance. There was no sign of either Frank Lloyd nor Carlos. However, they located his mother and her partner in one room. Understandably, both looked terrified. She was being comforted, and she wept constantly. The paramedics were brought in attendance.

'No person left the garden or the area. As I can see from the images and the thermal registers, we now have quite an audience.' Steve continued to follow commands from the operations' director until satisfied the target was not present. The images would continue to be relayed after all officers left the immediate vicinity. A final low-level check would be completed before the drone was returned to the parking area. It would, however, remain on standby.

April, accompanied by DI Peter Jones, needed to extract as much information as possible from the distraught couple in the quickest of times. Skeeter just needed to take a look around, being conscious not to disturb too much. After what had just taken place her input on the scene was likely to be minimal. Within fifteen minutes CSI would be on site for DNA sampling to search for a connection with the previous sites.

CHAPTER 30

'Thank you, Mr Rodgers. I've brought this to show you. It's evidence to prove to you what I'm telling you is the truth. Firstly, I want to show you the last page.'

He turned to the relevant page before offering it to Rodgers. He could see the grainy photograph of his partner, Debbie Sutch. He returned his gaze immediately.

'If you've fucking harmed her, I swear ...'

Frank held up his hand whilst shaking his head. 'You see, we two are no different. You would seek retribution just as I've done. Read it.'

'"Goddess – Guardian angels live forever."'

'You're a lucky man. Debbie is a kind, considerate woman. She was the only one that night to demonstrate any degree of human kindness. I would never harm one hair on her head. She cared about Carla too even though she knew about your ongoing relationship. She loves you. She keeps you from self-destruction. I think it was that factor that triggered all of this, flicked the switch somewhere inside my head. I don't know why, I don't.'

Rodgers let his finger run across the image of her face.

'Now turn the other pages. Some are not too pretty.'

Frank studied every expression on his face, particularly when Rodgers stopped at his own image. He noticed he did not linger but turned and looked at the other photographs and read the comments. There was clear revulsion as he stared at them.

'You're one sick, fucking bastard. You want to kill me?'

'Revenge is to be human. Revenge is said to be sweet. You know that, as you've practised it more than most. If I hurt Debbie, then what?' He did not give him time to answer. 'We waste time when you could be saving the life of an innocent man.' He leaned forward and turned the pages until Carlos's image stared back at Rodgers. 'You could save this man. You know him as Carlos. He worked with Carla. He knew Debbie too.'

Rodgers tossed the book onto the coffee table placed between them. 'What exactly do you fucking want? The police warned us to be careful as the killer would be unpredictable. We might be targeted next. They even offered protection. Debbie has it or so I believe.'

'God will protect her. She's safe.' Frank looked straight into his eyes. 'I want you to take his place. Take the place of Carlos.'

A long pause ensued.

'Are you brave enough to do that? Are bullies ever brave, Mr Rodgers? If not, I will leave here and simply vanish. No one will find him. They might find me but not for some time.' Standing, he moved towards the door. 'What's it to be?'

'How far are we travelling?'

'Fifteen minutes from here, but you need to change first.'

Looking at his feet, Rodgers moved swiftly around the table. 'You'll not leave here, you snivelling little gobshite, unless it's in a fucking box.'

As he spoke his arms grabbed Frank's clothing and drew him rapidly forward. Rodgers managed to connect his forehead directly onto Frank's nose and upper lip as his head was whipped forward. The target point exploded in a mass of blood, snot and teeth. They broke through the top lip, crumbled parts of which slid down his chin showing white in a mass of pinkish froth. Pushing Frank's lolling head away, he whipped it back again. His aim was now more accurate and the second head butt connected to the right eyebrow, splitting the flesh into a gaping, mouth-like wound. He had not finished. He threw him away yet again, only this time to gain the vital leverage that would allow his fists to pound the side of his head. The crunching thuds rained onto the collapsing man's face. Even when on the ground Rodgers knelt and continued his onslaught. Both fists now pummelled the small defenceless target. His animalistic grunts accompanied each blow, his hands themselves were bloodied and raw.

A slow burble broke from Frank's lips bringing with it blood red bubbles and pieces of broken tooth. His face had swollen rapidly and both eyes were almost invisible through the growing contusions and surface blood mass. The smashed nose no longer permitted the passage of air. He was slowly choking on his own blood. The incongruous thing was, a beatific smile appeared on Frank Lloyd's lips. Rodgers struck him again before he rolled onto his back, his dressing gown open and spattered. To an observer they were like two broken marionettes. Getting to his feet he stared down at the man. Fear flushed through his system as the adrenalin began to dissipate. Pulling him sideways he cleared his mouth before picking up his phone and dialling 999.

CHAPTER 31

April and Skeeter were about to leave the Mobile Control Unit when the call came through.

'Ma'am, he's at Rodger's apartment. He's called for immediate emergency medical support. It's on its way. The address ...'

Running to the car April tagged the postcode into the sat nav and the tyres protested as the car pulled away. The screen showed eight minutes as their ETA. The Saturday traffic was busy, but Skeeter forced the car through gaps and red lights. The first respond paramedic vehicle was parked outside, the strobes still blinking blue as they arrived. Another police vehicle pulled in behind.

The paramedic was performing CPR as they burst through the door. Rodgers was on the chair his dressing gown wrapped tightly around him. He seemed to be rocking slightly in concert with his breathing.

The sound of another siren became audible. The paramedic looked at Skeeter. 'Can you take over?'

Skeeter immediately knelt opposite and continued as the

medic shot through the door and down the steps. The supplementary oxygen tube inserted into his broken mouth to ensure a clear airway allowed her to concentrate on the chest compressions. April touched Rodgers who still seemed dazed.

'Let's go into another room and you can tell me what happened.'

Rodgers stood and collected the book from the coffee table before moving through to the kitchen.

* * *

On their return, the Incident Room was alive. One of the liaison officers was holding Rodgers in an Interview Room. April held the book wrapped in a clear forensic bag along with the contents retrieved from Frank Lloyd's pockets before he was placed in the ambulance. She had photographed the pages and transferred the images to the computer system.

'We'll hang onto these keys until we find Carlos,' April instructed the detectives.

Mason and the team observed as she went through the images and played the audio recording of Rodgers' account of the incident she had made on her phone.

'Vendetta, revenge. What's Frank Lloyd Millington's condition?'

An officer at the other end of the room pulled a face before announcing he was critical. He had been placed in an induced coma and been ventilated. He had severe head trauma and the diagnosis was that he was unlikely to survive beyond the day.

'So, where the bloody hell is Carlos?' Mason muttered as if thinking out loud.

'The only link we now have are these keys and his mother and her partner,' April responded, pointing to the bag on the table.

'And Gaskell, the father?' Mason mumbled as the thought came to him. 'Skeeter and Tony interrogate the father, April and Lucy, the mother, and Fred and Kasum, the partner. We need a location and we need it yesterday. Rodgers was convinced Carlos was still alive and somewhere within fifteen minutes of his apartment. He didn't arrive by car unless he took a taxi. Get onto that! I want an answer within the half hour.' He pointed to one of the officers. 'We'll calibrate travel on foot and by car for fifteen minutes from the flat. As soon as you have anything, call it in. Go! '

Skeeter and Tony sat opposite Gaskell. They informed him that Frank Lloyd had been apprehended but could not speak owing to his condition. There was little sign of any distress. They explained their urgency in locating a kidnapped male.

'Does he own any property? A garage, lock-up that would be hidden from view and large enough to store a car?' Skeeter leaned over the table as she asked.

'I don't know him. I told you that.'

'Your father, the builder, what about him?'

'He no longer builds, he's well into his seventies. He saw Frank, I believe, fairly regularly when he was growing up. He has what used to be a carriage house to the back of his place. Converted into garages and a store.' Gaskell realised what he was saying. 'He was going to convert them into a house but planning permission ...'

Skeeter immediately stood and leaned forward interrupting him mid flow. 'Address?' It was a demand and he knew it.

She scribbled it down and ran to the Incident Room. Mason watched her enter.

'It's as good a place as any. We can check this and leave the others just in case it's a false hope.'

'Take the keys and keep me informed all the way. We'll do the same, Wicca, if we get anything from the others.'

CHAPTER 32

The house, again Victorian, had been modernised. The outside red brick had in the past been rendered and painted white. A sturdy pair of iron gates opened onto the driveway to the right of the property where an old Jaguar was parked. Tony walked to the front door and rang the bell. Skeeter stood back. After a few moments an elderly man appeared and looked through the side window before coming to the door.

Tony had his ID ready. 'Mr Gaskell?'

'It is. I'll need glasses if you want me to read that. What is it?'

Tony looked down and noticed the man's slippers were on the wrong feet. 'Police officers, sir. DC Price and that's DS Warlock.'

He leaned out and looked across at Skeeter. 'Police you say? What do you want?'

'We've been speaking to your son, Craufurd and he informs us you have some garages at the back. We'd like you to check them for us now as a matter of great urgency.'

'Urgency, why, what?'

'I don't have time to explain.'

Gaskell went inside briefly and came out with a collection of keys. 'This way.'

They followed past the side of the house. Two further cars were covered with tarpaulins and the garden stretched some way to the side of the drive. The red-bricked wall backed onto the garden with narrow windows set high in two places. Gaskell went to the side door. 'Garages open onto a small yard and then the back lane.' Fumbling with the keys he searched for the correct one. 'Bloody thing's not here!'

'When was Frank, your grandson last here, Mr Gaskell?' asked Tony.

'A few weeks ago. Grand lad.'

Skeeter brought out the keys retrieved from Frank and approached the door. Checking the type of lock, she matched it with the keys. The one she selected went straight in. Turning it, she lowered the handle.

'How the hell did you do that?' Gaskell tried to look at the key in the lock.

Skeeter entered. The garage was gloomy. Little light seemed to penetrate the small wired opaque glass. She noticed the car first and pointed, directing Tony's attention. The smell was particularly pungent. Before her was Carlos. It was apparent that he had soiled himself. His head turned to look in her direction, his eyes frightened. She observed the red mark of the tick on his forehead as she moved quickly across. The stench was overpowering. To her right was a bench. Curved, discarded blades littered the surface. Part of a broom handle was held in the vertical from the vice.

Skeeter moved further into the garage and saw the remnants of the scarecrow.

'Bloody hell! Tony, call it in. We've found him. We need Forensics sharpish. Call an ambulance too.'

Gaskell said nothing as he looked at the stranger strapped to the chair. 'That's not Frank!'

Tony moved in and took Gaskell by the arm. 'You need to go back indoors. We'll see you when this is sorted.'

CHAPTER 33

Three days later

The Incident Room was being cleared as the team moved in. April and Mason were already there. Frank Lloyd Gaskell had passed away the day after the assault and Rodgers had been given bail having a manslaughter charge hanging over him.

April wrapped up the case. 'If the charge sticks then Frank Lloyd Gaskell will have got his wish, his plan, which I believe he had from the start. It will have been successful – "Just do it!" He certainly did. Vengeance can be cruel, but to turn it round so the main perpetrator ends up in prison is clearly the sign of somebody deranged.' She surveyed the room and found the two for whom she searched. 'Tony and Fred, you had a wager at the beginning of this case and neither of you won. That money can go to charity.'

Both men looked at each other, smiled and nodded their agreement.

'The DNA came through and it's been confirmed that

Frank was not Craufurd's son, so maybe he made the right call after all. The evidence found in his apartment will be reviewed, but it's felt as the woman is dead there will be little chance of securing a prosecution for rape. There might well be repercussions though for the hidden camera footage found, maybe even a prison sentence. I find secreting a hidden camera in the apartment's bedroom quite disgusting. However, that will be up to Smith if he wants to press further charges. It's clear he'll not be able to continue his role as landlord for some years to come, if at all. He'll be placed on the sex offenders' register.'

Carlos would continue to receive support but it was hoped that he would soon be back with Nicola in the salon. They had agreed to leave the mural in place for the time being. Carla would always be the one person who had brought him back from the brink no matter what others thought of her way of life. More than ever he contemplated the roles people played in the lives of others and how one action could change the path of others – some for the better, and some ...

Three weeks later

Skeeter and Trevor watched as Steve guided the drone until it was out of sight. Trevor's face was a picture of joy. Steve offered the occasional commentary. They had decided to fulfil their promise to Trevor and take him to experience a professional pilot at work. After an hour, Steve advised Trevor to look to gain a commercial drone licence and suggested he would offer all the help he could. It would give his life purpose and possibly a job doing something he truly loved.

It was at times like this Skeeter saw the difficult part of policing evaporate and her role within the community become more significant. Suddenly, it seemed so worthwhile and besides, she had decided she enjoyed Steve's company and would like to find out more about him than his ability to fly a drone.

THE GOLDEN GALLOPERS

A visit to this wonderful piece of Victoriana inspired part of the story and although none of the characters rides the carousel, the sound and its constant and steady motion play a key part in the sinister crime. If you do visit, do not forget to look for the one-legged diver, as he too is there, perched high on his pole looking down on the promenade.

Herbert Silcock's Victorian carousel is situated on Southport's promenade at the entrance to the pier. This historic and beautiful fairground ride was built in 1896 by Savages of King's Lynn. It was purchased by *Silcock's* in 1989 and took three years to restore fully, making its first appearance at the Shirdley Show in St Helens.

The Golden Gallopers weighs eighteen tons with a forty-two-foot diameter, standing eighteen feet tall. The three cockerels and thirty-three horses are each named after a member of the Silcock family and their friends. The three cockerels and the horses on the inside of the ride are original Anderson carvings and date to when the ride was first constructed. Wear and tear has necessitated replacements being made for the rest. However, the quality of workmanship in both the carving and painting of the replacements, is truly outstanding.

The Silcock family has been in the entertainment business for over five generations.

If you are in Southport, do pop along and behold the spectacle that can only be captured when watching an old fairground ride. You will still hear the sound of children's laughter.

MALCOLM

ABOUT THE AUTHOR

You could say that the writing was clearly on the wall for anyone born in a library that they might aspire to be an author but to get to that point, Malcolm Hollingdrake has travelled a circuitous route.

Malcolm worked in education for many years, even teaching for a period in Cairo before he started writing, a challenge he longed to tackle for more years than he cares to remember.

Malcolm has written a number of successful short stories and has more than ten books available (and more to come).

Born in Bradford and spending three years in Ripon, Malcolm has never lost his love for his home county, a passion that is reflected in the settings of several Harrogate Crime Series novels.

Malcolm has enjoyed many hobbies including works by Northern artists; the art auctions offer a degree of excitement when both buying and certainly when selling. It's a hobby he has bestowed on DCI Cyril Bennett, of his characters in the Harrogate Crime Series.

ACKNOWLEDGMENTS

Books are not written in a dark garret over endless hours – well not actually a garret, but many hours do go into each and every one. During the course of that work, many people are involved at various stages from the research to the proofing and editing, as well as those who read it to ensure it is not just a collection of paragraphs but a gripping and captivating crime novel. So, it is here that I must take a moment to express my words of thanks.

First and foremost, my thanks must go to my publisher, Hobeck Books; the team has worked so tirelessly in bringing this series to market. It has been a pleasure working within this supportive family.

A massive thanks also to a vital part of that family, the HART of Hobeck, the **H**obeck, **A**dvanced **R**eaders' **T**eam for their guidance and dedication.

As always to my wife, Debbie. She helps keep the motivation alive but sadly, she cannot do the same for some of my characters!

Helen Gray has worked with me now on a number of my

books and her sharp eyes check every word and sentence. Her skilful advice has been confidence-boosting and inspirational. Thanks, Helen.

Meeting the scarecrow at Johnson's farm was the catalyst for this story so sincere thanks to the man and wife team, Philip and Sandra Speakman, who create these fabulous human-like objects.

Writing is a lonely business but I have found people are always willing to offer a great deal of help and support whenever it is requested. So, thank you Carry Heap, Dee Groocock, Ian and Gill Cleverdon, Georgie Eadington, Lucy Teraoka and also to Malcolm and David at Reputation Menswear, Southport.

I have received tremendous support from authors this year so my thanks to Rob and Karen Ashman, Wes Markin, Tony Millington, K. A. Richardson and Robin Roughley.

All writers need their names whispered far and wide. This never happens magically but through dedicated readers who turn their reading hobby into a passion, either by writing reviews, administering social media and readers' groups or just by commenting on various social media platforms. Each and every one of you deserves a medal but I can only offer my sincere thanks. You know who you are. Bless you!

Finally, as always, last, but certainly not least, I mention you, yes you, holding the Kindle or the paperback, the reader, for without you I would not be here. Thank you for buying and reading this, the second book in the series.

If you have enjoyed it then please mention my work to friends and family, as word of mouth is the best way to encourage more people to read The Merseyside Crime Series and Hobeck Books.

Until Book Three

Thank you

MALCOLM

ALSO BY MALCOLM HOLLINGDRAKE

Bridging the Gulf
A thriller set in Yorkshire and Cyprus

The Harrogate Crime Series
Only the Dead
Hell's Gate
Flesh Evidence
Game Point
Dying Art
Crossed Out
The Third Breath
Treble Clef
Threadbare
Fragments

The Merseyside Crime Series
Catch as Catch Can

HOBECK BOOKS – THE HOME OF
GREAT STORIES

This book is the second in the Merseyside Crime Series, the first book, *Catch as Catch Can*, is published by Hobeck Books. There will be many more to follow after that (we hope).

If you've enjoyed this book, please visit Malcolm's website: **www.malcolmhollingdrakeauthor.co.uk** to read about his other writing, inspirations, writing life and for news about his forthcoming writing projects.

Malcolm is also the author of the acclaimed Harrogate Crime Series of which there are ten books.

Hobeck Books also presents a weekly podcast, the Hobcast, where founders Adrian Hobart and Rebecca Collins discuss all things book related, key issues from each week, including the ups and downs of running a creative business. Each episode includes an interview with one of the people who make Hobeck possible: the editors, the authors, the cover designers. These are the people who help Hobeck bring great stories to life. Without them, Hobeck wouldn't exist. The Hobcast can be listened to from all the usual platforms but it can also be found on the Hobeck website: **www. hobeck.net/hobcast**.

Finally, if you enjoyed this book, please also leave a review on the site you bought it from and spread the word. Reviews are hugely important to writers and they help other readers also.

Lightning Source UK Ltd.
Milton Keynes UK
UKHW021818040222
398214UK00007B/425